BME

BARBIE SCOTT

SUBSCRIBE

Text Shan to 22828 to stay up to date with new releases, sneak peeks, contest, and more...

WANT TO BE A PART OF SHAN
PRESENTS?

To submit your manuscript to Shan Presents, please send the first
three chapters and synopsis to submissions@shanpresents.com

"EITHER YOU GIVE up your supplier or I'll make sure your black ass don't make it out of here alive!"

"Fuck you! I ain't giving up shit you white piece of shit! Book me!" I yelled at the officer that stood in front of me screaming down my throat.

"Cap do you know that you could spend the rest of your life behind bars. And do you think BME will hold you down? Trust me their gonna move on with their lives and you will be forgotten all about."

"Bitch you could get yo fucked up weave wearing ass out my face. I ain't got shit to say without my lawyer present."

"You drug dealers kill me. Do you think a lawyer is gonna help you with this? We confiscated fifty keys of coke that was in your possession; so no. sorry. No lawyer is gonna help you. And you better hope I don't find any evidence regarding the murder that took place at the club a few years back." the cop threatened. "But you bet your black ass, I've been reaching." I laughed out letting him know I was unbothered by his threats. It's been 3 years and they ain't have shit, which means they won't find shit. Him and this corny ass bitch could get the fuck out my face before I caught an add charge for assault. I was five seconds away from spitting on these muthafuckas.

"He's not gonna talk. Let's book him." the bitch said then snatched me up out my seat. Her little sexy ass could have got the dick but instead she was on the opposite side of the field.

The officers walked me down the long hall and threw me into a cell. I shook my head as I took a seat because I knew this was about to be a long ride. I knew exactly how this shit was gonna play out and it was all a waiting process. They wanted me to give up Yanese and my team but I'd die before a nigga went out like a snitch. I know when Boss and Yanese find out that I had been careless, they were gonna be upset. But what I also knew was, Yanese loved a nigga and BME was a priority so she would do everything in her power to get me out. I laid my head back on the cold steal and everything tonight replayed in my mind.

I had just picked up the work and in the process of going to dump them my phone rang. It was this bitch named Dreyah that I've been trying so hard to smash. She had been playing hard to get talking bout she don't date niggas of my kind. Whatever that meant. So when my phone rang and I answered, the bitch invited me over; I bussed a U-TURN so fast. As fast as I made my U, all I saw was flashing lights behind me. A nigga was slightly nervous but I knew my rights. I had license, registration and insurance so them searching me was an illegal search. The officer that walked up on my car didn't even bother to ask any questions. He snatched me out and the way he handled me let me know shit was personal. I don't know what they had against BME but shit was about to get serious.

———

Sure enough, these pigs booked my black ass. Not even 24 hours later, I was on my way to the county jail. After going through more integration, they still couldn't break me so they slapped the band on me and threw me on the jail bus. These muthafuckas was being so fucked up they never even gave me my one call.

Pulling up to the jail, I stepped off the bus and was escorted into the building. The guard that was on the bus walked me to the cell. When we rounded the corner, the same officer that had arrested me was standing by the cell. He had a grimace ass look on his face and that shit wasn't sitting well.

When I entered the cell, a big skinhead was standing by the bunk eyeing me. The asshole officer hit him with a head nod and that shit too was off. I shook my head and walked over towards the bunk and suddenly I felt something sharp hit me in the side. I clutched my side and the hot liquid began to ooze from my side. Before I could speak, the skinhead began jugging my body repeatedly. I started getting dizzy and my body crashed to the ground. He stood over my body and stuck me in the neck, leaving the shank in me.

I looked over to see if anybody had saw this shit but niggas acted like nothing was going on. There was two more bunks in the cell and only one other inmate peeked from the covers. That nigga looked so scared I knew his ass wasn't even gonna try and help me. I turned my head towards the entrance of the bars and the same asshole cop that had pulled me over wore the coldest smirk. When he walked off, I knew right then I was set up and this muthafucka was gonna let me die right here in my cell.

As I laid on the ground, I could feel every ounce of blood in me pouring out onto the cold cement. My mind began to flash over my life. I couldn't believe I was gonna go out like this. I hadn't had any kids, I was leaving my team behind, and I didn't even get to fuck that pretty little bitch Dreyah. *Fuck!*

Veronica

Walking down the lengthy hallway, the only sound could be heard was my heels that clicked against the steel ground. In my long pencil skirt and suit coat, I knew I was looking good. I made sure to spray my *House of Sillage* perfume on every part of my body. I put an extra sway in my hips as I made my way to the sexiest nigga that walked the prison yard. Every day he had given me a hard time, but that wouldn't stop a bitch like me. This nigga was so fine, I wanted to bend over right there in that cell but I was determined. He was a complete asshole but I knew sooner or later I would win him over. All I had to do was follow up on my promise and he'd be free and I'd be getting dicked down by the king of New York.

When I made it to his cell, he was laid back on his bunk as if he was in a daze. He stared up at the ceiling; something he always did. I stood by the bars and watched him. It was crazy how he was locked up but looked better than most niggas on the streets. I don't know how he done it but his crisp, white shirt always looked brand new. He kept a pair of the latest Jordan's and his hair stayed freshly cut. I assumed he had someone come to his cell to hook him up because he never left it.

"Fuck you want?" he asked not even looking at me.

"Damn, how did you know it was me? You didn't even bother to look up."

"That stank ass perfume. A nigga could smell that shit a mile away." he finally looked over with his nose scrunched up. Ignoring his assholeness, I stepped into the cell.

"Why do you always give me a hard time?"

"Because I don't like pigs. So what is it that you want?"

"Look, I'm just trying to help you."

"You say that every time but a nigga still in this bitch. I guess you ain't trying so hard." he jumped down from his bed.

"I'm trying and trust me I'll have you out of here soon."

"What is it that you want Ms. Nelson? You want some of this dick huh?" he hit me with them cold eyes.

"Boy, I could lose my job."

"Shit, from the looks of it, it's like you're not worried 'bout yo job. You want some of this dick don't you ma?" He grabbed my ass and that shit had my pussy dripping. He breathed in my face and even his breath smelled good like Kush mixed with gum. I knew this nigga was getting weed indoors because me and Andrew were the ones bringing it in. This nigga was in here living like a fucking Boss.

"Look, I just wanna help you. That's it." I lied. He looked me in the eyes and he knew it was bullshit. He didn't say one word. Instead, he slipped his hand up my skirt. Without warning, he slid his finger into my opening and moved it in and out slowly.

"This pussy dripping so I know that's a lie." the slight moan escaped my lips and now I was ready to squirt all over his cell walls. When he moved his hand from inside of me, I damn near died. I wanted to feel him inside of me. I knew he was packing because he wore fresh grey sweats nearly every time I'd see him. And if it wasn't sweats it was Jordan basketball shorts. Dick print on display.

"You get me out, you get this dick. And trust me, it's gone be the best you ever had. Whoever that nigga is ain't fucking you right." he slapped me on the ass then turned to climb back on his bed. He was right; Melvin wasn't hitting me right. His little dick ass swore he was breaking my back out but a bitch was faking every orgasm. Sooner or later, I was gonna free this sexy muthafucka then Melvin would be left behind like a hooker wearing sweats.

I walked out the cell with hard nipples and a dripping pussy. I was gonna take my panties off in the car so I don't get caught up when I walked through the door.

Before I walked out completely, I turned to him.

"He was taken care of." I assured him. He nodded his head and without another word I headed out the building. I sighed because I had to go home to my weak ass husband.

Damn!

"WHAT THE FUCK you mean he's been moved?!"

"Ma'am, he's been moved to another facility."

"I've called every jail in New York and everyone said he was here. Booking information says he's here. Somebody better tell me something!"

"There's nothing to tell you. Now either you leave or I'll call back-up to escort you out." the minute she said it, I gave up. I would be damned if they took me to jail here at the fucking jail house.

Walking to my car, I was so fucking mad I had to light me a Newport.

Looking at the long line that had formed within seconds, I hit my cigarette as if it was my last. Smoking cigarettes was a habit I had picked up from my mother back in the days. Every time I went to light her cigarette on the stove, I would sneak and hit it. For many years, I had quit but right now, the way my life was going I needed it. Don't get me wrong, a bitch was living well off. Thanks to Yanese, I was set for the rest of my life along with my son that I had birthed by Trig. Trayon Edwards Jr. was 2 1/2 years old. And he too had everything he needed.

Just like Yanese had promised, three years ago I walked into my nail bar called Candy's Nail Trap. I had the best nail techs in the business and my shit was the most talked about. Life was good for me other than the games Trig played. He's a good baby's father and he takes great care of me, but I'm not dumb; that nigga a hoe like the rest of them. When I first met Trig was when we formed BME and the nigga had a baby mama that he fucked from time to time, so he said. But that bitch always said otherwise. Let her tell it, they been fucking since we met and even now that I have my son. I've never seen it with my own two eyes but you know that woman instinct, that little person on your shoulder that says, check his phone, stalk his shit, bitch he's cheating? Yeah, that bitch. I always listen to her and she's never steered me wrong.

"You have a call from 'Daddy'," my phone spoke breaking me from my daze. Seeing it was Trig, I answered knowing what he wanted.

"Hey bae?"

"Sup mama? What happened?"

"Shit they saying he was moved." I sighed.

"What! M, and it's some bullshit going on. I spoke with his sister and moms and they can't get a hold of him either."

"Same thing I said. Something really fishy."

"Man, just come home. We gonna figure this shit out."

"I'm on my way." I hung up the phone. Something was hella crazy with this situation. It's not like Cap to not call. Now I don't know he this nigga was under protective custody from snitching or was he in trouble but shit was sus.

⊏⊐

Pulling up to one of the traps, I noticed Brent and Marcos' car across the street. I quickly exited my whip so I could see what the fuck we were gonna figure out. Cap is like a brother to us so I knew this shit wasn't sitting well with the team.

"Sup sis?" Marco said as I stepped into the house. Even though Marco was a total asshole he was my boy. He treated me like a sister and I felt sorry for the women he dealt with because that nigga attitude and mouth was foul as fuck. He didn't care what came out of it.

"Hey Bro." I gave him a slight hug.

"Sup Big ol head ass girl." Brent laughed and pounded me on top of my head.

"Shut yo water head ass up." I playfully hit him. Brent was my boy. He was more of the flirty, laid back type. Sometimes his flirting was over the extreme because that nigga would flirt with me and Yanese right in front of our men. Although they took it as he was playing, they were complete fools because had we given him a chance, he would smash for sure. I couldn't blame Trig for being jealous because Brent was sexy as hell no lie. But what it didn't matter because my baby was just as sexy.

"Man, I hope this nigga ain't telling!" Trig shouted on a more serious note. I knew he did it because he always hated the way Brent flirted. He was jealous as fuck but what he failed to realize was, I wasn't into *Loving The Crew*.

"Man, that nigga ain't telling. I just hope he's okay. Something don't seem right. We gone wait a couple more days; if he doesn't call then I'mma send one of my bitches to holler at the warden. Until then, I'mma hit Boss and have him holla at Peters." Marco said referring to the officer that was on our payroll. I hopped like hell Cap called because I didn't want to have to bother Yanese and Boss with this shit. Ever since they married and had another child, they both pretty much fell back from the game. Boss still dibbled and dabbled but he left Marco pretty much in charge. Everything in the organization came through Marco.

After chopping it up with the fellas, Trig sent my ass home like always. I hated the way he treated me now. He was extra overprotective of me and that shit got on my nerves. This nigga met me in the

Trap and now he wanted me to leave the *Trap* alone. I understand I have a child now, but damn, I was still a part of the team.

When I walked through the door, my phone was ringing non-stop. Because I had so many bags in my hand, I couldn't answer it. Dropping the bags on the kitchen floor, I went into the living room to retrieve my purse. When I pulled my phone out and looked at the caller ID, I frowned my face because this bitch was a pain in my fucking ass.

"Bitch, why are you calling my phone?"

"Because our man ain't answering his. Tell that nigga while he playing house with you, our daughter needs shit."

"I ain't telling him shit. Fuck you and your ugly ass daughter hoe!" I shouted hanging up.

I hated to be so evil but this bitch was constantly pushing my buttons. When I first got with Trig, I had problems out the bitch. Then, suddenly, it was like she fell off the face of the earth. About eight months ago, the bitch resurfaced and I was more than sure it was because he was fucking her again. I wasn't no fool. When bitches act out, it's because a nigga dicking her down and selling her dreams. I swear if I found out it was on.

Pushing the keys into my phone, I was furious as I dialed Trig's number. The minute I heard his voice on the other end, I went in.

"Nigga, you better call and check that hoe. I swear this bitch gone make me catch a fucking case!"

"What the fuck is you talking about?"

"I'm talking about your ratchet ass baby mama. Bitch just called my phone. I swear you better check that bitch before I do and if I do it's gonna be way worse." I hung up the phone before he could speak. I was so mad my lips and hands trembled. I plopped down on the sofa to calm my nerves because right now I was ready to go beat this hoe up.

Trig

I swear this bitch Jasmyn was gonna be the death of me. She knew exactly what she was doing. Because I rarely paid her any attention, she knew how to get attention out of me. She knew pulling a stunt like this would have me on my way to her crib and that's exactly why she did it. I had too much shit going on right now to be caught up over bitch shit. Don't get me wrong, I loved Candy and I loved my BM, but both these bitches could get on my last nerve.

Candy constantly bickered about Jas and Jas bickered because I was with Candy. When I first got with Candy, Jas and I were together. Candy pretty much came in and took a nigga. I left Jas high and dry and basically started another life. I didn't mean for Candy to have a baby and us fall in love but it happened. It was simply supposed to be some in-house *'Trap Love'* where we fuck and go our separate ways. When Candy told me she was pregnant, she was so excited that I couldn't bring myself to shit on her and tell her get rid of it.

Then, there was Jas, the bitch that held a nigga down since I was a typical corner boy. I loved Jas but she was a straight loony bin and that shit turned me off. The reason I still fucked her from time to time was out of guilt because of the way I had done her for Candy.

When Jas found I had a new bitch, she threatened to tell Candy. I stopped fucking with her to protect Candy's feelings but shit hit the fan when Jas found out I was having another baby. She did everything in her power to get to Candy. One day, she saw Candy at the doctor's office and tried to fight her. Because of Jas, I had detail with Candy because I knew what Jas was capable of. However, Candy's pregnant ass ended up slamming Jas on her head. She called my phone tripping but what was I supposed to do? I couldn't let her crazy ass harm Candy, especially while she was pregnant. Ever since, she been coming for Candy, she wouldn't jump bad.

Pulling up to the four bedroom crib that I once shared with Jas, I dreaded going inside. I deaded my engine then headed to the door. I stuck my key in and prayed my daughter wasn't here so she wouldn't have to hear us fussing. More than likely, Jayla wasn't here because her mother always left her with her grandmother.

"Oh, you run yo ass over here when that bitch get in yo ass." she fussed right went the door opened.

"Man, why you always gotta be on some bullshit? You always starting shit, Jas." I stepped into her face.

"And I'mma keep starting shit. You just up and left me for some random bitch and had a baby. Nigga, I'mma always cause havoc in y'all life! You not about to be happy with this bitch while I'm over here miserable and lonely. You got shit fucked up!" Jas was screaming and started crying. She know I hated when she cried so she did that shit on purpose. But that shit wasn't gonna work today.

"Man, shut that shit up. Yo ass always trying to play victim like you wasn't the reason I started cheating. You pushed me to the arms of the next bitch." I lied. I had to make her feel guilty.

"But you could have come to me before you just went and fucked the next bitch."

"I tried, Jas, but you was always too busy."

"Nigga, I have a career." she cried again. She was speaking the truth.

As crazy and ghetto as Jas was, she had a good job. While I stood on the corner, she went to school. We held each other down up until she graduated and landed her gig. She worked as a dentist and she was always busy. If she wasn't at the office, she was buried in books. The communication slowed down and even the sex.

Marco and I were boys so he offered the position working for Montana to me so I was always in the streets. That's how Candy and I became so close because we were always around each other. Candy was hard to resist. She was sexy as a muthafucka with flawless, choco- late skin. Her body was banging like she had work done but she was all natural. Spending every day in the trap with her turned into a night of her bent over the couch with her ass in the air. The minute I stuck my dick in her, a nigga was hooked.

"I just want you to come home and be with me and our daughter." she cried knocking me from my thoughts.

She wrapped her arms around my waist and she knew what she was doing. She had on these little ass shorts that was riding up her ass. My heart said go home to my wife, but my dick was saying just put the head in nigga then go. Before I knew it, I had Jas bent over in the kitchen holding the sink for dear life. I loved doggy style and with all the ass Jas had, that shit had my dick hard as fuck. Every time she threw it back, I could see her juices covering my dick like a glazed donut. This was one of the reasons I couldn't stop fucking Jas. Her pussy was good and she was a straight squirter. Sex with her was always wild and fun, unlike Candy; she was turning into a boring fuck. She always wanted to fuck from the side on some lazy shit. I loved Candy with all my heart and I swear if I lost her I'd die. Which is why I had to keep Jas happy so she wouldn't run my wife off.

By the time I walked into the house, Candy was laying in the bed sleep. I quickly jumped in the shower because I didn't wash up after the episode I had with my BM. A nigga couldn't walk in the house smelling like fresh soap. When I was done, I climbed into the bed and pulled Candy next to me. I prayed like hell she didn't want to fuck because a nigga nut sack was on E.

Jas and I had fucked for hours and by the time I was on my third nut that shit took forever to come out. When Candy didn't budge, I was happy as hell. My mind drifted off to Cap, and I was starting to worry. Something about the whole situation wasn't right. I prayed like hell he was just being moved around and couldn't make a call because if that nigga was telling, I knew for sure the whole BME was going down.

This nigga knew everything about the operation. Shit, he was a partner instead of just some random worker. I couldn't phantom the thought of him telling because I knew he would take Boss and Montana down right along with us. Cap was really like a brother to me and everyone else. But I also knew a nigga that never been in that type of situation could possibly fold. Unlike Cap, Marco and I, we had been to the pen. We knew what it was like to be interrogated and even walk that yard. Cap was the youngest of all of us so he had never experienced anything like this. We was getting major money, and I was sure we'd have some heat from the pigs. However, we moved smart. If the police was onto us, it had to be somebody telling.

3 / MARCO

IT WAS the night of Brent's birthday so we were in club Savvy turnt up. He didn't want a party so we were pretty much just chilling. We had bottles and strippers in our section so we were on our boss shit like always. Trig had finally left Candy at home so we were able to enjoy our night out. Don't get me wrong, I loved Candy like a sister but because she was a part of the crew she came out with us all the time. Most of the time, I could tell Trig was annoyed because he couldn't relax and be himself. We couldn't shoot the shit in front of her and not to mention this nigga had to always be on his ten toes.

Sis was bad, hands down, and no matter where she went niggas flocked to her. So this nigga kept his hand on his waistline and his eyes on his bitch. At all times. A nigga like me was happy I didn't have those problems and I'm sure I never would. I didn't have no bitch trying to tie me down, however, I did have a stable of bitches. I was single and getting money so me slowing down would never happen. I was enjoying life and bitches was a distraction. They whined, begged and always wanted to be up under a nigga. I didn't like all that lovey dovey shit. I wanted to fuck and keep it pushing, which is why I didn't have a main bitch now.

"Damn, you can't speak." I heard Nana's annoying ass voice. I looked up at her from my seat then looked over at Brent. I knew it wasn't nobody but his ass that okayed security to let this bitch behind the ropes.

"Fuck out my face Nana."

"You a rude muthafucka." she said eyeing me.

I looked past her trying to avoid eye contact. Of course she was with the rest of her thot ass friends but there was one I had never seen; or should I say fucked. I fucked Nana a few times but the bitch was too clingy for me. She was doing shit like she was my bitch so I cut the hoe off. Out of the five friends, I smashed three and Brent's nasty ass smashed like nine. That nigga a fuck anything.

Anyway, this little chick I saw standing here now was the odd ball out the crew. She looked innocent like she didn't belong. But I knew more than likely if she was with these sack chasing hoes, dick bandit bitches, she was in the same boat. *Her little pretty ass could get it though.* She reminded me of the singer Cassie. She had slightly tight eyes and some pretty ass pouty lips that I imagined wrapped around my dick. I stood up and walked up on her then grabbed her head. I ran my hands through her hair and I didn't give a fuck about messing her shit up.

"Boy, what the hell." she whined pulling away from me.

"I was just trying to see was it all yours." I sat back down and continued to ignore them.

"Y'all have a seat." Brent called them over. All of them walked over to where he was and took a seat. I watched as the Cassie look alike sat down and began scrolling in her phone. As much as I didn't want to look at her I couldn't help myself. Out the corner of my eye, I could feel Nana watching me so I made sure to ignore her and piss her off at the same time.

"Y'all hoes, I mean ladies want something to drink?" I asked trying my hardest to be nice. The only reason I was being generous was because this pretty little bitch was with them. I had never seen her before so that made me curious to know how the fuck she link up with them?

I got up from my seat and walked over to the chick. I snatched her phone out her hand because she had me all the way fucked up.

"What the fuck is your problem?"

"You don't hear me talking to you?" I asked holding her phone.

"I ain't no hoe, so, no I don't hear you talking. And can you give me back my phone please." she stood up and tried to snatch her phone.

"You'll get it when I give it back. Now do you want something to drink or not?" she looked unsure but shook her head up and down. I walked back over to where the liquor was and poured baby girl a drink. When I handed her the glass, I could feel Nana burning a hole in me. But like I had been doing, I ignored her ass.

"Um, so, Morgan is the only person you see right here?"

Morgan? Yeah, that shit fit her. "And your point is?"

"You get on my fucking nerves Marco." I ignored her last statement and continued looking at the strippers. Every now and then I would sneak a peek at Morgan's sexy ass. I was trying my hardest not to look thirsty but when I saw Brent rub her leg I damn near lost it.

"Morgan!" I called out to her making her look up. She was smiling all in this nigga face but that shit was about to end. I had first dibs on her little fine ass.

"Bring yo ass over here." I demanded then turned back to the strippers. After about five minutes, I noticed she had not listened. "If I have to say it again I'mma come drag yo ass." again I focused my attention back on the bitches. I could hear chatter from the rest of the girls but I didn't give a fuck.

When Morgan brought her ass over to me she was pouting like a damn kid. I tried my hardest not to look at her because I didn't want to submit to her. I didn't know this girl from a can of paint but something about her was different. I was just talking all that shit about relationships and not even twenty minutes later I was over here acting like a crazy boyfriend. Normally, when hoes came around us, they were like starstruck groupies and we wasn't even no stars. But

Morgan, it was like she was unfazed by what a nigga had or who a nigga was.

"You're not my man nor my fucking daddy nigga. I don't even know your fucking name and you demanding shit like I belong to you."

"First off, watch yo fucking tone. Second, I'm not yo nigga yet. Third , if I was your daddy you'll be at home and not in no fucking club wearing no little ass shit like this. Got niggas feeling all up on you and shit."

"Who the fuck are you?" she rolled her eyes.

"Chill with the fucking attitude. You wanna be like them hoes." I pointed to Nana and her friends. "Then take yo ass back over there," I told her annoyed. All she needed to do was sit her ass down and chill. I handed her back her phone and waited for her to shake. When she didn't move, that told me she was interested. She moved into me a little closer and no lie that shit made me feel better.

For the first time tonight, I was able to relax. It was like baby was my calm and I'd only known her two hours. We tripped off the strippers and even made a little small talk. I couldn't get too in tune with her because I couldn't get too comfortable. Although we didn't have beef with nobody, I still had to be on my ten toes; especially in this type of environment. In this game, you just never know when a nigga will try you. I was now doing bigger and better things so I understood that with more money came more haters. After the whole, King Cam thing, shit had wind down, so I wasn't worried bout that situation.

Niggas already hated my hustle. I had been doing this shit since a youngin. Even when I was just a corner boy, barely getting money, niggas was still hating. I bled the block non-stop while niggas were buying cars and flossing for bitches. I was busy stacking my bread.

When Yanese addressed me about helping her form a crew, that was all the opportunity I needed. I knew Yanese from my cousin Dajah and imagine my surprise when Dajah mentioned what Yanese wanted. I had met Yanese a couple times and she was corny as fuck brah. I don't know what the fuck happened in her life because it was like overnight she had turned straight savage. In no time, I made Yanese a easy few mill. She fell back and let Boss take over which was fine with me.

I actually liked Boss. That nigga was a true gangsta and a Boss for sure. When I was a youngin, I knew all about Boss. I used to see him roll up the block in all kinds of foreign whips and I always said, I'mma be like that nigga when I get older. Therefore, I knew I wouldn't make it by spending. Nigga thought because I rocked a pair of sweats and wife beaters I was broke and that's exactly what I wanted people to think. Now, here I was, a 23-year-old Boss. I had enough dough to retire and run my business. Right now, I owned a skating rink because there was only one and that shit had too many white people in there for me. We needed some shit for the urban community so I took it upon myself to give back.

On weekends, it was 21 and over because I served alcohol. On Monday and Wednesday, it was what they called kitty land for kids 2 up to 13. And on Tuesday and Thursday it was Teen spirit night for 13 to 18 years old. Sunday I had gospel night because my gee moms begged me for it. I told her ass she was wrong. Because the night before we were drinking and smoking weed, the next day niggas in there had the holy ghost. But I couldn't argue with her. Don't ask me why I picked a skating rink because I didn't know how to skate for shit and I for sure would never try. Like I said I did it for my community. Everywhere you went in New York, there was clubs. We needed something for the kids to enjoy. So with that said, I was the proud owner of *Hot Wheels* Skating Rink.

"So are you gonna ever tell me your name? I mean you keep calling me your future wife." Morgan said bringing me from my daze. I was so lost in my thoughts I damn near forgot she was here.

"Marcell," I looked over at her then focused back on the crowd.

"Marcell." she said like she didn't hear me.

"Call me Marco." I told her because nobody called me Marcell but my mother who is now dead.

"Are you always like this?" she shoulder nudged me.

"And what's that?"

"Just so demanding. You're...."

"We ready to go." Nana walked over and stood in front of us with her arms folded across her chest. It was evident she was mad with her hating ass. I just hoped she didn't scare Morgan away from me. I knew when they left, Nana was gonna give her a ear full.

"Don't you see us talking." I shot ready to turn up on this bird head bitch.

"Okay and we ready to go Marco."

"Okay bye." I shot her my evilest glare.

"I'm not leaving my friend with you."

"Bitch, you saying it like I'mma let something happen to her. Fuck on before I slap yo ass Nana." I sat back down. This bitch was about to piss me off and she knew how I was when I was mad. I didn't hit women, but I would embarrass the fuck out of a bitch in a minute.

"It's okay Marcell. I'mma just go. I'm kinda tired anyway." Morgan said then fake yawned.

"Yeah, aight. I'll see you tomorrow. Nana, take her the fuck home." I wasn't playing. Nana only rolled her eyes. The girls left and me and the fellas continued to do us. I gave Nana enough time to get home because I was about to pop up on that ass. She needed some act right and I knew exactly what that was.

Two hours later, I was pulling up to Nana's crib out in Yonkers. I jumped out the car and knocked on the door.

"Who is it?" she asked from the other side of the door.

"Man, just open the door." she swung the door open with her fake attitude. I walked in and went straight to her bedroom.

"Why you here?"

"Stop acting like you don't want me here Nana. Take that shit off."

"I'm not fucking you. You disrespectful as fuck."

"How's that?"

"Fuck you mean how's that? You all in my fucking friend face."

"Why do it matter yo? You not my bitch."

"You always hollering I'm not yo bitch but you stay up in this pussy like I'm yo bitch."

"Just take that shit off." I ignored her.

"Oh, now you wanna fuck me? You wasn't worried about me at the club. That shit wasn't cool Marco."

"Man, I'm out; you bugging." I got ready to walk out the room, and just like I knew, Nana began begging me to stay. I turned around trying my hardest not to laugh. Nana was thirsty as fuck but hey, a nigga wanted some of her fire ass head. Okay, I'm lying. I just wanted to know who the fuck Morgan was and where she'd come from. And after, I'd dick Nana down and gon bout my business.

I PULLED my phone from my purse and I wanted so bad to call Marcell, but I had no way to reach him. Ever since the night at the club I had been thinking about him something serious. A part of me wished I had given him my number so I could see if he would call me. I mean, it was pretty clear he was a busy man, because I could tell he was a hood nigga. Most hood niggas hustled and when they hustled, they hustled hard. Although he was a complete asshole, everything about him turned me on. His arrogance was appealing in a weird kind of way. He rocked a white tee with a fur coat and that was the sexiest shit ever. He wasn't that tall but he was taller than me which was at least 5'9.

He had smooth butter brown skin and lips was sexy as hell. He had a slight mustache I could tell he kept trimmed regularly and his eyes looked like they told a story. It was something about the way his eyes looked at me. I could tell he was not only a killer, but he had a troubled past. I could vividly see him pushing his shoulder-length dreads out his face, then hitting me with a look of lust. When I took my seat next to him, I brushed up against his gun on his hip and that shit made my panties wet right there in that club.

Marcell was the type of guy that my family forbade me to date. In their minds, I was gonna marry a doctor or a lawyer but that was their dream not mine. I was done with those types of men. They were pushovers and with my attitude that's exactly what I would do. No matter how old I was, my family was still overprotective of me. Thank God they were back at home. My family had moved from New York just so they could be near me in school which was stupid as fuck. They were so overprotective they wouldn't even let me live on campus.

Now that I'd graduated, you'd think they would cut me some slack but hell no; they were still on my back. I was down here for the summer and the only reason my parents wasn't chasing behind me was because my father had just had knee surgery so my mother stayed behind with him. I was staying with my aunty while on vacation and even my cousin Cambree had come down from Miami. We were having our annual family reunion soon which was why Cambree had come.

Cambree was the overprotective big cousin also so I had to keep shit away from her too. She couldn't stand Nana ever since we were kids. She always said "that girl too hot and her nasty ass gone have a baby by twelve," and Cambree wasn't lying. Nana was fast as hell and although she didn't have a baby, she had a million abortions and fake miscarriages. I say fake because any nigga she liked, she would fake a pregnancy and when it was time for her to show, she would fake a miscarriage. However, Nana was my dog for so many years so Cambree didn't have to like her; I did. I knew if she found out I was in a club and especially with Nana she would tell my parents.

Cambree always had an input in my life. It was pretty stupid if you asked me because all she dated was dope boys and even had a baby by one. She was the last person that could judge me so if she ever found out I was all in Marcell's face, I was gonna rub her life in her face.

"Hello." I answered my ringing phone.

"Heyyyy, Hoochie," Nana sang into the phone.

"Sup, Hoochie."

"Girl, nothing just left the Rucker's."

"Oh, what was you doing there?"

"Marco wanted me to come watch him play. They had a game." she said trying to rub it in my face.

"Marco?"

"Girl, yes. After the night at the club, he came over and we fucked. He said he was just *on* you to make me mad because he heard I fucked Brent." Even though Marcell wasn't mine, I kinda felt jealous and was now in my feelings.

"But you did." I rolled my eyes annoyed. Nana had fucked with the entire BME as she referred to them and bragged about it like it was cute. I didn't see shit cute about it when her ass was still broke. All she talked about was BME this and BME that and how much money they had. But what was crazy, she was fucking them all and still broke.

"Sooo. He don't gotta know that." she said bringing me from my thoughts.

Beep.

My other line beeped.

"Umm, I'mma call you back; my line is beeping."

"Aight, hoe, call me back too." she said but I hung up. After what she had told me my little day was ruined. So more than likely I wouldn't be calling her back.

"Hello." I answered reluctantly.

"Why it take you so long to answer the fucking phone?" I knew his voice all too well. I tried my hardest to not smile.

"How you get my number?" I tried to act unmoved.

"Do it matter. Where you at, though? I need to see you."

"For what?"

"Fuck you mea... look, ma, I'm not bout to do this with you. You drive? If so, meet me in Bed-Stuy at the courts."

"Damn, didn't you just finish balling?" I asked because of what Nana had said.

"Huh?" he asked puzzled which let me know it was a lie.

"Nothing. Never mind."

"Man, jus be there at 4:00pm sharp. I'll be on the BIG yard." his rude ass said then hung up. A part of me was nervous but the other part of me was excited. I couldn't wait to ask this nigga about him and Nana. If he thought he was gonna be messing with me and my friend he was crazy.

I don't know why, but if it was one thing about Nana, I knew she was a liar. Once before she had liked this boy that was on me, and she told me they had sex. The boy put her on blast in front of all his boys including me and she had the nerve to be mad. Talking bout, why would I tell him what she said? She was upset because she lied on her pussy and that was her bad. We didn't speak for months but of course that didn't last because she wanted to borrow my red Jordan 12's.

I lifted from the bed excited and began digging through my suit-case. Even though it was a sunny day, it didn't mean it wasn't cold. In NY, the summer was nothing like summer time in Atlanta. Out here in August it would only get to 90 degrees maybe. In the A, it was 90 in the damn winter. So after settling on some denim jeans and a red Supreme crop, I pulled out my red and black Jordan 11's then headed for the shower. I couldn't stop smiling the entire time.

———

When my Uber pulled up to the yard, my legs were trembling. The whole way here I pumped myself up and I swore I could handle this shit but I wasn't fooling nobody. I've never dealt with a guy of Marcell's caliber so this shit was all knew to me. I tried to play the tough girl that fucked with dope boys but that wasn't even the case. I was very attracted to them but, truth be told, my parents wouldn't let me out their sight long enough to explore the hood. The closest thing to a thug I fucked with was my ex Rashad.

He wore the saggy pants but his brother was the one who sold drugs. Of course, him being the most popular guy in school had went to his head. Like, who does that in college. Nigga was acting like he was still in high school. He left my ass high and dry because I wasn't having sex. You heard right. Here I was going on twenty-two years old and never felt penetration. Rashad finger-banged me a few times if that counts but I was always scared to go further. I talked a good game and even popped my ass like I was taking twelve inches of dick but that shit was cap at its finest. Nana and the rest of the girls thought I was having sex. The only person knew I was a virgin was Cambree. The only reason I lied to Nana was because I was tired of being teased.

When I stepped out the Uber, I made my way towards the crowd. It was so many niggas, I stopped in mid-stride. I took a seat on the benches and tried to act like I was all in my phone. I kept looking up to scan the crowd for Marcell and, right when I did, I spotted him talking to some chick. Wheat ever the girl was saying had him smiling, which was odd because I didn't even think the nigga ever smiled. Finally, he looked up and we held each other's gaze. I slightly smiled then dropped my head. If he wanted me, he had to come to me.

I busied myself on my phone for about twenty minutes and this nigga never came. Finally when I went to my Uber app, he must have sensed it because he walked over to where I was seated.

"Let's roll up outta here." he said and turned to walk away. Already annoyed, I did as told and followed him to the lot. I was curious to where we were going because we had now made our way to a brand new McLaren 720 S. It was beautiful. I never seen one in person and it was much nicer.

"Is this your car?" I asked as I climbed inside.

"Don't tell me you're one of those." he looked at me with a slight head shake.

"One of those? What's that supposed to mean? And if your referring to me asking about your car, nigga I ain't no fucking gold digger. I don't give a fuck about what you got. I was just asking because I've never seen one up close." I rolled my eyes. I wasn't feeling his little comment so I chose not to say shit else to him.

A little over and 45 minutes into the ride, Marcell and I haven't said two words. I felt him looking at me but he remained quiet. Pulling up to a house in Westchester County, I couldn't say I wasn't impressed. I wasn't gonna tell him how nice the home was because then he would really think I was a sack chaser. One thing Marcell didn't know about me was I came from money. My entire fucking family was rolling in dough from my cousins to my grandparents. My parents too had nice cars and we lived in a seven bedroom home that was paid off. However, Marcell didn't need to know that.

"Get out." he said then slammed the door. I had to woosah because this nigga was five seconds away from seeing my other side. I got out the car and walked up to the door. His rude as had already disappeared into the house so I guess that meant let myself in. When I walked in, I knew his mother or someone had to live here because it was decorated nicely like it had a woman's touch.

The house was huge as hell from where I stood. Marcell had vanished into the house so I didn't know where the hell I was going. I waltzed down the long hallway until I heard the shower running inside a room. When I walked in, I assumed it was his room because it was decorated in dark colors and there was a plaque on the wall that read BME. I took a seat on the bed and nearly sank in. It was so huge and soft I wanted to lay down.

Looking around, I admired his decor. It was nice. He had a marble scheme going that had a deep gloss. His dresser matched his headboard nicely. Laying on his dresser, I noticed a bracelet that said BME that was flooded in diamonds. Alongside was his watch that's also eye-catching. Just looking at his Bulgari Magsonic watch, I could tell he had taste because my father had one just like it. The watch cost nearly 500 grand.

Ten minutes later, Marcell had come out the restroom wearing only a towel. His back was still slightly wet and got damn this nigga was fine.

"Marcell, why are we here? I'm not fucking you." I told him to make sure we had that understood.

"Man, ain't nobody trying to fuck you. I had to wash my ass. And if I did want to fuck you, I would have took you to a room, fucked you, then dropped yo ass off." that statement alone hurt my feelings. I swear if I didn't hate his ass, now I did.

"You know what, take me the fuck home and you ain't never gotta say shit to me. You are so fucking rude with yo hoe ass." *Why the fuck did I say that?* He shot me a look like he wanted to slap the taste out my mouth.

"Why I gotta be all that Morgan?"

"Because you are a hoe. You fuck my friend and now you're trying to get with me but ain't shit happening. I wouldn't fuck you with her nasty ass pussy."

"Man, ain't nobody fuck that girl."

"She told me nigga. You know it's crazy you were all up on me at the club just to go home and fuck her. That's some trifling shit." I yelled mad all over again.

I tried to storm out the room but he grabbed me before I could. I looked at him with so much hate and it was weird. It was like love at first sight with this nigga. I've never felt like I needed a man to want me. But with Marcell, it was different. I wanted him to want me bad. I knew dealing with a guy like him, I would end up hurt but for some reason I wanted to take that chance. However, I couldn't let my feelings get wrapped up into him for two reasons. One, he constantly reminded me he was single and two, because I would be going back home soon.

"First off, I ain't touch that girl and if I did I'm single Morgan." *Exactly my point.* I shook my head. I guess he could tell I was somewhat hurt by his last words because he began clearing that shit up.

"But check it, you here because a nigga like you. I don't bring women to my crib ma. From the first day I saw you in the club something told me you were different. If I'm wrong, my bad but you don't seem like you belong with the people you associate yourself with." He said referring to Nana and her friends. "Answer me this ma. How many niggas you fucking?" he asked eagerly.

"I'm not fucking nobody."

"Don't lie to me."

"I'm not lying to you."

"So when the last time you had sex?"

"I don't know a year ago maybe." I lied with a shoulder shrug. He didn't say another word. He nodded his head up and down as if he was contemplating my answer.

A part of me felt relieved that he hadn't fucked Nana so I was now more relaxed around him. For the rest of the evening, Marcell and I chilled in his home and watched movies. He asked if I had to be home, and I lied and said no, so I guess I would be crashing here. Well, I didn't fully lie because I didn't have to be home, but I was more than sure my Aunty would tell my parents and I would have to hear their mouths. The way we were vibing it may be well worth it.

"Ооннн, shit, daddy right there! Oh, yes, stick it in my ass."

"You want it in the ass?" I sised. She didn't have to tell me twice. I pulled right out her pussy and slid into her ass with no Vaseline. This bitch was a cold freak.

"Ughhhhh!" she screamed out as I slid my whole dick inside of her.

"Ohh, shit, here it come ma. Here it come." A nigga wasn't in her ass five minutes and I was already about to bust. I shot a fat load up in her ass and caught a fucking cramp in the process.

"Don't move. Shit, don't move." That shit hurt like hell. When the pain finally stopped, I rolled over off her and laid there breathing hard like I had run a marathon.

"I'm not done with you." she said then climbed on top of me.

Just feeling her wet pussy brought my dick right back to life. I helped her slide down, then I folded my arms behind my head and let her ride me like a Kentucky derby. Little mama was a straight beast. She slid up and down my pole then moved her hips side to side then up and down again. Her titties bounced with each move and right now, I wanted to suck on them muthafuckas. I made her lean forward so I could devour them pretty muthafuckas. I used both hands to squeeze them together so I could suck on both at the same time. She bounced on my dick not missing a beat.

When she tried to kiss me, I moved my face then grabbed her waist. I slammed her down onto my dick wit so much force. I began moving from the bottom because I wanted her to cum. This session was over for me because I had to meet the fellas at Hot Wheels in less than an hour.

After finally making her cum, I lifted up to jump in the shower. Once I was done, I was pissed to see she was still laying in the same spot.

"Come on, ma, I got shit to do." She smacked her lips like that shit was gonna make my plans change.

"Is this all you wanna do is fuck me?" she asked as she slid into her dress. I shook my head because her ass didn't even bother to go wash her pussy.

"I mean, what else could we do?"

"How about you treat me like yo bitch instead of some hoe."

"Why would I treat you like my bitch Mercedes? Let's be real, what could we possibly do with each other other than fuck. You got a baby by the homie."

"So what, fuck him. I wanna be your bitch."

"What you mean fuck him. Man, I ain't trying to get caught up in no shit with you and Boss." I lied. I wasn't worried bout shit; I just needed her to think that.

"It's too late nigga. What you think he gone say when he find out?"

"He ain't gonna find out and yo stupid ass bet not ever say shit." I told her then went into my wallet. I counted out a band then tossed it to her. This all she wanted so I made sure to give it to her. I grabbed my keys off the dresser then made my way to the door. She was hot on my heels so I tried to move as fast as I could.

"Go home, ma." I told her then hit her with a fake ass cheek kiss.

"I'm staying here." she shot with her arms folded like that shit was gonna do something.

"Aight, and you gone be here by yourself. I'm going home tonight." I told her then walked to my car. Her ass could stay all she want. This house was used strictly for pussy so it didn't maske me none. I had a fat crib to go lay my head at.

I know what y'all thinking; this a cold nigga. You damn right! I don't give a fuck who you are; you come flaunting that pussy around me I'm taking it. Don't get me wrong, though. I know I was living foul fucking Mercedes but so what. This bitch wanted to be my bitch bad but hell no I wasn't no fool. Mercedes had a track record that I heard about a long time ago. I never knew who the bitch was when Boss always talked shit about her so imagine my surprise when I found out.

One night I was at the club and she was eye-fucking me from across the room the whole night. I tried to ignore her only because I had another shorty with me. The minute baby went to the restroom, Mercedes came over and slid her number in my ear right along with her tongue. I knew then she was a cold freak because her ass was too damn bold. I put my number in her phone before Shauntay came back then told her I'd hit her up. I really didn't plan on it, but shit, she beat me to the punch. The shit she said in the text made me drop Shauntay off and buss a U-Turn for the pussy.

I fucked her ass that same night and been fucking her ever since. One day, the bitch found me on Instagram so I liked a few of her pics then start looking through the rest. When I stumbled up on a picture of her and Majesty, I couldn't do shit but shake my head. I mean, come on, it's a million Mercedes in the world but that picture confirmed which Mercedes she was. *Damn.*

To be honest, I wanted Yanese. I wanted that bitch bad. She was cute with her shy ass but most of all she was a Boss. When I found out she was fucking Boss and King Cam, it really didn't surprise me. She was moving shit in these streets like a nigga so why settle for less. When she passed the empire to Boss, I couldn't front, we were really eating but that didn't stop the temptation. One slip-up from that nigga and Yanese gonna be mines. Just like he had lost her to Cam, I knew I had a chance at her; I just needed this nigga to fuck up.

Mercedes

I know what y'all thinking. After everything I've been through and put Major through, I'm still around doing wicked shit. You damn right because a bitch gotta get her coins, and not to mention some dick. Speaking of dick, you damn right I've been fucking the shit out of Brent big dick, sexy ass. When I first started fucking him, it was out of spite. As time passed, I fell more and more in love and wished he'd stop playing and make me his bitch. I knew when Major found out, he would be upset but oh well. He was living well off with his bitch and they played house with my son.

Major ended up with Majesty because a bitch like me was trying to *do her*. He gave me half a mill and told me to get lost and you damn right I did. I had left New York for two years and ran off to California. However, that shit didn't last. I ended up hooking up with a guy from Compton and that nigga had me into all types of shit. I went to the sunny state for beaches and relaxation next thing I know I was hitting licks and walking the hoe stroll.

Shaking my head, this nigga had basically took all my money and pimped on me the moment he knew I was in love. He was sexy as fuck and a straight gangsta. I mean, he wasn't as rich as Major but he was getting his money because he ran a few crack spots.

Make a long story short, one date to come up, turned to two and next thing I know, I was a full blown prostitute. One night, I met a trick who turned out to be a dope boy and took him to a hotel. Because my so called pimp CJ was following us, he knew exactly who he was. He came up with this bright idea to set the nigga up, so I did it. I told him my brother wanted to buy twenty bricks, I sucked him up, and he was meeting us at a secluded location. When he showed up, CJ robbed him but let the nigga get away. Months later, CJ was killed and my face was hot so I had to get away.

Of course, I came back to New York and everything I went through I blamed my baby daddy. This nigga was happy and living good meanwhile I was a California fugitive. Thanks to that bitch Yanese, I lost everything I had, which was my initial reason for hating her so much.

After hating her for so long, though, I finally let it go because she had stepped up to the plate to raise Majesty. She slid me money without Major knowing so I sucked up my antomosity with her. You can't beat them, join them, were my thoughts every time I looked at her. All that innocent shit was bullshit. Imagine my surprise when I found out that bitch was Montana. I just knew I was about to come up on a new baller and I would have Major mad, but nahhh; it just had to be this bitch.

When I tell y'all that slick hoe was pushing so much weight she put most of these so-called hustlas to shame. That was another reason I became envious. But like I said, the bitch started looking out for me. Anywho, enough with her and Major. I'm back, I'm taking my son back soon, and Major gone have to cough up another house. For now, I'mma fuck the shit out of Brent and lay low.

Laying in Brent's bed, I was being hard-headed as hell. He told me to leave but fuck that I was gonna be here until he came. He claimed he was gonna go home to his little *hoe house* but that nigga couldn't resist this pussy. Brent was single as a muthafucka and soon he would be tired of being a hoe. When he was ready, I was gonna be the bitch that waited with open arms.

What the fuck? I thought watching his snapchat.

Brent was in a club with two bitches sitting on each side of him. Then one of the girls reached over and whispered something in his ear. He nodded his head then took a sip of his cup and looked back into the camera. The next snap was him walking but the camera was facing one of the chick's ass. Her ass cheeks poked from the bottom and it wobbled as she walked. They walked into a room that was dimly lit. I instantly became jealous so I flung my phone across the room. This nigga had me fucked up. I mean, I know he was fucking all kinds of bitches but damn, he also knew I followed his snap. I lifted from the bed and decided to go shower to cool off. I couldn't wait for him to come back because I was gonna dig a mud hole in his ass.

"THE PAPERWORK IS IN!" Andrew shouted eagerly.

"So that means..."

"He's up for an appeal." we both said at the same time.

"You like him don't you?" he asked looking at me through beaded eyes.

"Nooo." I blushed at just the thought.

"Lying ass. I know you like him, but if I were you, I'd leave the thought alone. Messing with a guy like him is dangerous."

"I know, I know. I don't like him like that. I just want to help him." Andrew shot me a look as if he knew I was telling a bold-faced lie.

"We're gonna do what we can but don't get your hopes up."

After talking to Andrew, I quickly went to my car and headed for Rikers Island. I eagerly walked down the halls excited about the news I had received today. When I got to his cell, he had his head down and he was playing chest. Crazy part about it was, he was playing alone. I studied him for a moment and he was in deep concentration.

"You gone just stand there like a creep and watch me?" he never lifted his head to look at me. I nodded for the deputy to unlock the cell and once he did he left to give us some privacy.

"Hello to you too." I closed the cell behind me.

"What you want ma?"

"I came to give you the good news." I said and he finally looked up at me.

"I'm waiting."

"You're going up for your appeal." I smiled hoping he would lighten up. Instead, he looked off into the air and I swear this nigga was a sexy ass weirdo. After a few seconds of silence, he looked over at me and smiled.

"Good looking, ma. A nigga appreciate you." he nodded his head. Without warning, I took it upon myself to walk over to him and grab a handful of his dick. He stood to his feet but he didn't object. I began stroking it through his sweats and it began to rise right in my hand. *Damn this nigga got dick,* I thought as my mouth watered.

"Bend over." he told me with so much force. I did as told and hiked up my skirt.

Waiting for him to enter me, I wondered what the hell was he doing. I looked back at him and he was sliding a condom on. *How the hell this nigga get condoms in here? And who the hell he fucking in here that he needs them?* I thought feeling slightly jealous. *That bitch Angela,* I thought. I knew she liked him because I could tell how she always looked at him and I swear one day I could have sworn I saw that bitch come out his cell. I've been knowing Angela for years. We had done the academy together and even had a few college classes together.

"Ahhhhh." I growled out because this nigga had damn near ripped me a new asshole. Talk about knock me out my thoughts. We gone get back to Angela later on. Right now, I needed to get this dick I had been waiting on for years.

"Come here ma. Stop running; ain't this what you wanted? Bring that ass here." he was holding me around my waist pulling me towards him. As bad as I wanted the dick, I didn't expect it like this. I wanted it to be sensual. I wanted him to kiss me from head to toe but instead he was banging my back out with so much force. I can't lie, though, his shit thick and long and I could feel him touching every last wall inside of me.

"Ohhh, shit!" I screamed out on a verge of an organsum. As he pumped, he was growling. The way he tilted on his tippy toes I could tell he was gonna cum soon.

I knew after this, this man was gonna get me in a world of trouble. His dick was magical. I've never felt no shit like this except Boss Major. Boss was the only nigga that fucked the life out of me. Now for the second time in my life, this man was making me see stars.

"I'm about to cummm. Shit, I'm bout to cumm." he growled in my ear.

"Ohh, I'm cuming tooo... ohhh shit Daddy!" I screamed as I felt my juices run down my thighs. He quickly pulled out of me and bust into the condom that was damn near hanging off. I hurried to lower my skirt because I didn't want to take the chance of getting caught. I don't know why but for some reason I couldn't look at him. I walked towards the cell and my legs felt like they were gonna give out. I tapped on the cell so that I could be let out. The deputy walked up and nodded his head then unlocked the door.

"Ms. Nelson." he called out to me. I turned around slowly and was met with his piercing eyes.

"Yes." I spoke shamefully. I wasn't ashamed I had cheated on Melvin or that I had fucked an inmate. I was ashamed that this man was heaven sent. His dick was bomb on top of him being sexy as ever. I knew now I would fantasize about him more than I already did.

"I'll be seeing you soon right?" he asked knocking me from my thoughts. He wasn't asking because he wanted some of this pussy again; he was asking because of his appeal. I shook my head yes then stepped out. I walked the hall and headed straight to my car. Before I pulled off, I laid my head back on the seat and sighed hard.

"Get it together Vee." I pep talked myself before driving off.

When I pulled up to my house, I exited the car and reluctantly went inside. When I stepped in, the smell of beer reeked through the air and I knew then that Melvin was on one tonight. I walked into the living room and found him sitting on the couch with a colt 45 in his hand. I shook my head because this nigga was a straight bum. The once dboy, with good looks and swag to make any girl's head turn, was now a leeching, beer head, bum.

When I met Melvin, he was the shit. I was still healing from a broken heart from Boss Major and Melvin came in and picked up the pieces. We started off good then out of nowhere he began to change. It's like he got too comfortable with my money and stopped hustling. He was now living off me and that shit was starting to drive me crazy. I swear I hate that bitch Yanese. Had it not been for her, I'd still have Boss and be living the good life. But it's cool; I had something for that man stealing hoe.

"I'm glad you home. I missed you baby." Melvin stood up and walked towards me.

"I'm not in the mood Mel." I walked towards the room with him on my heels.

"I've been waiting on you and this sweet pussy all day." he rushed his hand up my skirt. Before I could jump back, he had already brushed his hand across my clit.

"You nasty hoe!" he charged me and knocked me to the ground.

"Stop it!" I cried out but he continued to punch me.

"You trifling bitch! You- come - in- my- house- smelling- like- another- nigga!" With each word he punched me with so much force.

"I haven't done anything." I cried. He hit me again and again and before I knew it, I blacked out.

"Oн, my God, what the fuck did y'all do to him?! How the fuck he comes to jail and all of a sudden he's dead. I swear if I find out y'all did something to him I'm killing shit.

"Ms. would you like me to detain you for threatening an officer?"

"I don't give a fuck. I want the arresting officer's name! And if I don't get it, my lawyer will!" I was screaming at the warden. This bitch had me fucked up. How the fuck my bro come to jail and dies. That shit don't sound right and it ain't adding up. I crossed my hands over one another and I was gonna wait until somebody told me something. I wanted the police report from the night he was arrested and best believe I was gonna look into the arresting officers.

"Here you go, ma'am." An officer walked over with the police report. I snatched it out her hand but I wasn't done.

"Where is his body? I need to ID him?"

"We're waiting for his next of kin to come identify the body ma'am. You could leave your number and you'll be contacted when we know it's him."

"He don't have any damn family. I am his family!"

"Sorry, ma'am, there's nothing we can do. There's an Ella Johnson listed on as his next of kin."

"Ella is his grandmother and she's dead."

"We have to find that information out first." She walked away from me and ignored my outburst.

"You know what? I'm going to just call my lawyer. You bitches in here playing games and my muthafucking brother is dead." I stormed off.

I was so frustrated I couldn't do anything but cry. The thought of Cap being dead was too much to bare. With all the memories I contained, the one that stuck out the most was his big smile. Cap had a set of pearly white teeth with a smile to light up the earth. Although he was ruthless, he was nothing like Trig and Marco; he was so chill and humble.

Walking to my car, I looked up into the sky and said a silent prayer for my brother. Cap wasn't my biological brother but shit we had been through so much together. BME was a family and we had a unity that no one could stand in front of. I knew when I broke the news to the fellas they were gonna lose it. Especially, Trig. I hopped into my car and headed to the spot that the fellas hung out at. I knew they were there because they were always there. These nigga were crazy because no matter how much money they made, they visited the spot frequently.

When I pulled up, I quickly jumped out and headed inside. I bypassed one of the workers who had unlocked the dead bolt. Marco was sitting at the table counting money and some cute brown-skinned chick was sitting by him on her phone. Trig had just emerged from the back and he looked at me as if he could tell something was wrong.

"Where's Brent?" I asked because he wasn't in his usual spot on the couch playing the game.

"You know Brent; he somewhere chasing some pussy." Marco said as if he didn't do the same.

"I need to holla at y'all." I told them but eyeing the chick that was sitting next to Marco. He caught the hint and stood up."

We all walked to the back and I closed the door. I looked at the fellas and before I could say a word, I burst into a fresh set of tears.

"What's wrong, ma?" Trig grabbed me and I collapsed into his arms.

"They killed him." I cried out.

"Killed who? What you talkin bout CeCe." Marco said calling me by the nickname he gave me.

"Cap! They killed Cap." I blurted out. Marco drew his gun and Trig turned around and threw his hands over his head. I don't know if he was crying but I could tell he was hurt.

"Who killed him?"

"The police, Marco. I went to the jail and they finally told me he was dead. They said they couldn't give me the cause of death or any more info because I wasn't his next of kin." The moment the words left my mouth, Trig stormed off and moments later I heard the door slam.

Boom!

The sound of a hard thump caused me to nearly jump out my skin. Marco had put a hole in the wall with his bare fist. He began pacing the floor as warm tears began to fall from his eyes. I haven't known Marco my whole life but I've known him for years and it broke my heart to see a thug cry.

Marco was the crazy, but calm, didn't give a fuck nigga from the squad. Because he was the one to introduce us to Montana, that made him captain of the ship. He was so raw and rugged that I never in a million years thought I'd see the day he would break down. Seeing him cry made me cry harder. Not only did we lose a friend; we lost a brother.

The light knock at the door made me look over. Without invitation, the door slowly came open. The girl that was with Marco had walked in with a worried look.

"Marco, is everything okay?" her soft voice spoke and her eyes held so much worry. Whoever this chick was, I could tell she was in love with Marco just by the way she looked at him.

"Man, just go Morgan!" he yelled at her and I could tell he hurt her feelings.

"But..."

"Do what the fuck I said!" he shouted again.

She looked at me before walking out and I felt so bad for her. But right now was not the time so I understood how Marco felt. I lifted from the ground and went to go find Trig. When I walked outside, his car was gone and the chick was standing in the front like a lost soul.

"Just give him some time. He's going through something right now." I called out to her. She turned around and thanked me with a head nod. I went back inside to console my brother but thoughts of Trig were heavy on my mind. I knew he was capable of anything and that's what worried me the most.

⸻

Trig

"They kill one of ours; we kill one of theirs!" Marco shouted to everyone that sat around the table. I watched him as he spoke and I could tell he meant business. His eyes were bloodshot red and appeared as if he was half drunk and all cried out.

"It ain't like we could take it out on the streets, so we gone make every muthafucking pig feel it. The report that we got from Candy has the arresting officers by the names of Andrew Cummings and a Veronica Nelson. Now, I don't know if they had anything to do with his death but at this point I really don't give a fuck. I got something for Cummings but for this bitch Nelson, I got a plan. If anybody here scared of the pigs or wanna bitch out, get the fuck from around me and don't bother to come back. He looked around the room but nobody said a word. Well at least until this dumb ass nigga Snake spoke.

"Nobody scared Marc, but how the fuck are we supposed to kill cops?" Marco shot the nigga a look of death and knowing Marco, that's exactly what was about to....

BOOM!

Before I could even finish my thoughts, I heard a single shot go off. I emptied the blunt into the ashtray without even looking in Snake's direction. I knew that nigga was dead and that's where he needed to be. Right now, we were on a mission and the way I was feeling, anybody could get it.

Cap wasn't just anybody in the camp. He was in command just like Marco and myself. It had been almost a week since Candy told us what had happened and the pigs were holding onto his body. With a little money and Peters, Candy was finally let in to ID him but they still were being dicks about releasing him to the morgue. I was ready to bury my nigga and go to war.

Ring...Ring...Ring....

The sound of my ringing phone made me look down. Of course, it was my nagging ass baby mama. When I looked up, I was met with Candy's eyes and they were not pleasant. I tried to turn my head but yet and still I could feel her burning a hole through the side of my face. When Marco took his seat at the head of the table, I stood to my feet from my seat which was the other head of the table.

"Everybody know how I felt about Cap. That nigga wasn't just anybody; that nigga was a brother to us. Marco right, it's time to go to war with the pigs but first I wanna bury my nigga peacefully. After that, bodies dropping and pigs is crying. Everybody know he ain't have no family but that nigga is our family. Marco and I are gonna handle all the arguments and I want everybody to give they bread and sizes to Candy so she could pick out our suits and colors. West, for now, you gone take over all the spots Cap ran." I looked over at West and he nodded his head. "Slim you gone cover all West spots and Cane you gone have to run shit on your own without Slim. since it's already eleven, everybody take the night off and we gone start fresh in the morning.

Bam! Bam! Bam!

Somebody was beating on the door. Everyone jumped to their feet with their guns drawn. Big Rick, the guard, opened the door and I couldn't do shit but shake my head.

"Nigga, I know you see me calling you." Jasmyn walked in with her annoying ass. She rolled her eyes at Candy and Candy did the same.

"I'm busy, Jas, and didn't I tell you stop popping up to all my fucking spots."

"Why, because of this bitch?" she said and rolled her head at Candy. Candy jumped to her feet but I was about to end this shit before it got uglier.

"I ain't gone be too many of yo bitches hoe!"

"Candy, sit the fuck down!" I told her before she could move.

"Yeah, sit the fuck down like a good dog supposed to do." Jas laughed like shit was funny. Before she could get it all the way out, I yoked her ass up.

"This better be good because I swear I'm five seconds away from snapping your fucking neck."

"Get yo fucking hands off me." She was screaming and tugging at my hands that was wrapped around her neck. I could hear Candy laughing in the background. When I finally let Jas go, she was coughing dramatically like I was really killing her.

"Nigga, you gone do me like this for this bitch?" she began crying.

"I ain't doing you like shit for nobody; you just hard-headed."

"Fuck you mean you ain't..."

"Not right now Candy." I held my hand up for Candy to silence herself. Being the stubborn ass girl she was, she stormed out the meeting, making sure to slam the door. I just shook my head because I knew it was gonna be some shit when I got home. I swear these two chicks were gonna be the death of a nigga.

"I'm bout to take my baby to the hospital; she's running a fever while you sitting here with that bitch." Jas said and walked away. I knew what she was doing, and I wasn't falling for her shit. She knew how much I loved my daughter so she knew I would be by her side until she got better. Last time this happened, I was at Jas' crib for two days trying to break my baby's fever and when I finally got home, Candy had a nigga shit packed by the door.

"Go handle that, my nigga. I got it from here." Marco told me as if he could read my thoughts. I just shook my head and walked out the door. This was gonna be a long night and I knew how shit was gonna play out.

When I pulled up to the hospital, I sat in the car and called Candy back to back. Her dumb ass didn't answer so I knew she was pissed. Before I made it to the hospital, I had drove past the crib to see if she was home and she wasn't. I already knew her ass wasn't nowhere but at Montana's crib because she didn't have any friends. Ending the call from Candy's voicemail, I called Boss. Moments later, he answered and without asking I could hear Candy's loud ass in the background.

"Yeah, she here nigga." he answered the phone laughing.

"How you know that's what I wanted?"

"Nigga, how you think? Because her and Yanese in there gossiping about yo ass now." We both laughed.

"Aight, keep her ass there for me bro. I'm at the hospital because my daughter had a fever."

"Aight, my nigga. I send my love to yo little mama. I got you."

"Aight, good looking."

"Yo ass bet not be calling that nigga telling him I'm here."

"Girl, ain't nobody telling on yo ass." I heard Candy and Boss going back and forth before the line disconnected. I felt a lot better knowing Candy was there because for sure she wouldn't take a nigga to Boss' house. Not saying that Candy will cheat but I knew sooner or later she was gonna get tired of my shit and there was no telling what she would do.

I exited my car and headed into the hospital. Jas had another thing coming if she thought I was gonna stay nights at her crib. I was gonna make sure they kept Jayla in here so I could be right here with her. After getting the info I needed from the nurses' station, I headed up to the room. Before I stepped in, I shot Candy a text telling her I love her then slid my phone back into my pocket. I pushed the door open and couldn't do shit but laugh. Jas wasn't even here. Her mother was sitting next to the bed and Jayla was sound asleep.

"I got it from here, Ms. Booney."

"Okay, son. I'm tired as hell." She stood to her feet. I didn't bother asking where her daughter was because that shit really didn't matter. All that mattered to me was my daughter and I was now by her side.

"WHERE YOU BEEN? Let me find out you got a new boo?" Nana said fishing for information.

"Girl, I been in the house sick with the flu." I lied. Okay, I didn't all the way lie. I was actually in the house and I was sick, just not with the flu; A bitch was love sick. For an entire week, Marcell and I were together every day and on the phone. Then, the day we were at his Trap, he tripped out on me and embarrassed the hell out me in front of some lady. Granted, the lady was nice, but that shit hurt my feelings. I was just showing concern.

Ever since that day he hasn't called. Right now, I hated myself for falling for him so fast. The time we've spent together showed me another side of Marco. I got to learn who Marcell was. Don't get me wrong, I loved the Ruff and Thugged out Marco, but under that hard exterior was a boy with a heart. He told me about his family, how he was abandoned and his mother's passing. When he spoke on his granny, it was like his world would light up. He also mentioned wanting kids one day and even moving out of New York. I wanted Marcell in the worst way. And even though he hasn't asked me to be his girl, he treated me like I was his.

"Bitch, you just zoned out on me!" Nana screamed through the phone.

"My bad." I giggled trying to play it off.

"So how you feeling? I got somewhere I want you to go with me."

"I don't really feel good."

"Man, yo ass already been MIA for a while and not to mention you leaving soon to go back to school." she begged.

"Okaaaay, damn. Let me get up and slide on something." I told her and lifted from the bed. I quickly disconnected the line before she could get another word in. As bad as I didn't want to go, she was right. I was gonna be leaving soon so the least I could do was chill with my friend.

———

"Bitch, where we going?" I looked over at Nana who was driving like a bat out of hell. She had her Migos blasting and she was smoking a blunt. This girl was wild. She had her hair in a high bun which was why she didn't care about my hair blowing in the wind and fucking up my curls.

"To see my boo." she squealed then faced the road. I left it alone and focused my attention towards the clouds. I was still kind of heart-broken but right now I was glad Nana had gotten me out of the house. Marcell had me all the way fucked up so, right now, fuck him.

About twenty minutes later, we pulled up to a run-down looking home. There was a basket out front and constant drug addicts walked up and down the street. There were a grip of guys on the porch and a few in the middle of the street playing basketball on a homemade looking court. Although it looked gutta as hell, I was a bit excited to be around some hood niggas. Now don't get me wrong, a bitch was a bit nervous because I've never been at a trap house that looked of such. The trap house I went to several times with Marcell looked much better than this and there was not that many niggas hanging out.

"Now, don't get in here with that bougie shit Morg."

"Girl, boo. I'm not bougie and, trust me, I could handle myself."

"Yeah okay. Well, I hope yo ass can handle if the police kick the door in or some niggas come by busting." she giggled. I rolled my eyes and ignored her ass. We walked up the stairs and as we approached the door some nigga grabbed my hand. I quickly pulled away but tried my best not to be rude about it. I wasn't on no stuck-up stuff but Nana had already informed me not to talk to the first guy that tried to holla because he might have cuter homies. Without hesitation, Nana grabbed my hand and pulled me into the house.

"Damn, like that Nana?" the guy yelled out but we kept walking. When we got inside, the house was just as packed as outside. There was a few girls inside and a house full of niggas.

"Sup, West?" Nana said to a guy smoking a blunt at the table.

"Sup, Na?" he nodded then looked up at me. My eyes fell onto his chain and I damn near fainted. His plaque read *BME* in diamonds.

"Damn, what's wrong, you nervous?" he said looking at me. I guess it showed that I was fidgeting.

"No, I'm fine." I fake smiled.

"Y'all want some drank?" he asked still looking at me.

"I don't..."

"Yeah, what you got?" Nana quickly responded.

"Dark, clear, champagne, whatever you want?" he said then stood to his feet.

"You could give us clear." Again, Nana answered for me. I shot her a look and she arm shrugged me and whispered. "Lighten up."

Trying not to be the party pooper, I took the drink and sipped it. I liked drinking sometimes but most times I would pass. I hated the way it made me feel in the morning. When I did agree to drink, it would be an Adios Muthafucka. I really liked the taste.

"This nigga got me fucked up." Nana said looking over the rim of her drink. I followed her eyes and I damn near spit out my drink. Marcell had walked out the room and he wasn't alone. He was with some brown-skinned, curly haired girl. No lie, she was really pretty. What tripped me out was, why the hell was Nana tripping. *Did they really mess around?* I thought because she was looking pissed. Let Marcell tell it, he had never fucked with her like that. My heart fell into the sole of my sneakers just watching him with the chick. She was smiling all up in his face which was odd because he was a mean ass muthafucka.

Finally looking over at me, Marcell and I locked eyes. He looked surprised to see me. The chick noticed our stair down and grabbed at his hand. I quickly turned my head like I wasn't moved by his presence. I tried to focus my attention elsewhere but the way Nana was looking only added to my hurt.

▭

We had been here for almost two hours and Nana was getting on my last nerve. She was trying her best to start shit with Marcell's little boo but I could tell she was scared. Marcell would beat the brakes off her ass. Every now and then he would come over and ask if we needed anything but I ignored his ass each time. Nana kept making slick comments but he ignored her just as I did him.

I was now slightly tipsy and feeling good and I had to keep reminding myself that he was not my nigga. Speaking of, some cute ass nigga walked through the door like he owned the place. Dressed in a simple black T, some jeans and black Giuseppe's, his chain blinged and his hair was freshly braided. His caramel complexion was bomb but, no matter what, he wasn't fine as Marcell. I looked over at Marcell the moment I had the thought and now my feelings were hurt again. I stood here for hours watching him entertain some chick like I wasn't shit. I was now ready to go.

"Who's your friend?" The cute guy walked up and asked Nana. She began smiling like always and that shit was beginning to annoy me. I noticed how any nigga that tried to talk to me she would basically push me into his bed. What was really crazy was it was always the niggas with money. It's like she didn't understand I wasn't no gold digger. True, I didn't want a broke nigga but there was some cute, rich, niggas out here that weren't flashy.

"I'm Morgan." I extended my arm to shake his hand.

"Sup, ma. I'm Cane." He smiled exposing his bottom grill. He began talking to me but everything he said was a blur. My eyes landed on Marcell who was eyeballing us with so much aggression. He was basically ignoring the chick because he was so busy in my and Cane's mouth. I turned my head and focused my attention on Cane who was now standing right in front of me.

"So where you stay?"

"I'm from ATL; I'm only out here on vacation. I live on campus." I lied. I didn't want to say I live with my parents because they are too damn scared to let me live on campus.

"Oh, is that right. So I'm bout to have me a college wife?" he smiled.

"You ain't bout to have shit!" his voice boomed from behind us.

"Take yo ass to the fucking car Morgan."

"Nigga, you got a lot of fucking nerves." I stood my ground.

"Oh, this you Marco?" Cane asked and threw his hands up.

"Yeah, nigga, so if you ever see her that's me." he told him and shoved me outside.

"Wait, what the fuck is going on here? The girl that was with Marco walked up.

"Man, go sit yo ass down." he told her annoyed.

"Naw, it's good. I'mma just leave." I said and snatched away from him.

"Just go to the car and wait for me Morgan."

"Fuck you mean wait for you? What she waiting for?" The girl rolled her neck in Marcell's face.

"Do y'all mess around?" she walked up on me.

"Bitch, you ask him. Don't question me about shit." I stood up to her.

"Oh, so y'all is fucking? You a scanless ass nigga. You just came out the room from fucking me and now you in this bitch face." she said and right then and there, I knew there was no sense in arguing with this chick. For the third time, Marcell had crushed my little spirits. I couldn't act out the way I wanted to because of Nana's nosey ass. So I kept my mouth shut.

I stormed down the stairs and went to get in Nana's car. I locked the doors because I didn't want to be bothered. Moments later, Marcell came out and Nana was screaming all up in his face. At this point, Nana and the other chick could have that nigga. I turned my head to act unmoved by the two but slowly I was dying inside. I tried so hard to keep the tears from falling because I refused to show weakness especially in front of Nana. When she finally climbed into the car, I didn't say a word.

"Do y'all fuck around or something?" Nana asked getting into the car.

"No Nana."

"Well, you keep saying that but I see different. I hope you not trying to fuck with him because we stay fucking, Morgan, and I'm trying to give that nigga a baby."

"You good. I don't want him." I lied. I looked back out the window and Marcell and I locked eyes. This time, something was odd. He wore this look like he was sorry but the feeling of the moment told me this would be my last time seeing him. I swear, after today, I was gonna get over my feelings for him and never look back. I was leaving soon and I couldn't wait. I wanted to get far away from New York as possible. For the first time in life, I understood why my parents tried to keep me away from D Boys. They had money so they came with bitches and bitches came with problems. *He'll just break my heart anyway; Right?*

"Nigga, what's up with you? You been off yo square lately."

"Nothing, I'm good Boss."

"Man I been around you long enough to know when something wrong. I mean I know this shit with Cap got you bugging but nah son something telling me it ain't got shit to do with Cap." I sighed as I rubbed my hand down my face. I couldn't believe shit was that evident.

"It's this chick man." I shook my head. "A nigga really feeling her but I don't know."

"What you mean you don't know? Shit, by the looks of it she gotta be mad *ill* because yo ass don't love no bitch."

"She is *ill*. And that's the problem. I wanna fuck with her but I don't know how to love a bitch. I'm not no Romeo type nigga. You already know me yo."

"So what's up with her?"

"Shit, last time I seen her she came to the trap off Main and I had just finished fucking Mira. Lil mama took it like a gee but I could tell I fucked her up. I mean, I didn't mean to, but shit I didn't know she was coming. A nigga ain't seen her since." I rubbed my hands down my face. "Now I hear she leaving day after tomorrow to go back home." I looked out the window into the night. It was like something in the air peaked my interest but wasn't shit there. I was in deep thought.

"If you really wanna rock with her don't let her get away from you. You only get one chance at real love lil bro. Trust me. I was that same nigga. I had hoes and not to mention I wasn't supposed to fall in love. Nigga, I met Yanese and one look at baby, a nigga was in love. I cut all my bitches off and trip this, she had a husband at the time. I didn't give a fuck. I was determined to make her mines. So like I said, don't let her get away from you because you on some prideful bullshit or because you don't wanna be in love. Everybody need somebody, Marc."

Just the thought of Yanese and Boss' relationship had a nigga in a zone. They shit was rocky in the beginning but now they had a solid foundation. The kind of love anybody in the world would want. "Now if I was you, I'd stop her ass from leaving. Hogtie her ass and throw her in the trunk." Boss said and we both laughed.

Shit didn't sound too bad after all. Thinking it over, I just nodded my head. One thing about me was I listened. I didn't mind soaking up game from a real nigga and especially a nigga that been through it all. Boss was the only nigga I ever looked up to and one thing about me was I didn't admire no nigga. I was that nigga but with Boss, I had to give credit where it was due.

"What's up with that shit shit?" he asked bringing me out my daze.

"I got Brent on it."

"Yeah, get on that asap. I just hope he don't fuck it up. It's something bout that nigga I don't really like. But because that's y'all boy, I fuck with him. You just watch that nigga, Marc. Lately, he been on some weird shit and I just got a bad feeling about him."

"I got you, Boss." I understood exactly what he meant. It was something going on with Brent that wasn't sitting well with me. And now that Boss had said it, it only confirmed my assumptions. We had a cold plan, however, I hope Brent ol tender dick ass didn't fuck shit up. That nigga always acted like a gigolo but that pussy whipped ass nigga was a pillow talking ass sucka. I kept Brent around because once upon a time he was solid. It's like since he been eating good, he been moving different. Nigga been on some high power shit like he was bigger than the program, but this empire was mine so there wasn't no nigga bigger than me; not even Trig and that was my right-hand.

"Ah nigga bout to slide to the pad." Boss grabbed the duffle bags and went to open the door.

"You not gone count it?" I asked because we had a crib where we kept work stashed and counted up the day's profit.

"Nah. I trust you nigga." he said and climbed out. Just hearing the words made a nigga feel good. One thing about me, I was a trust-worthy nigga and I'd die protecting my loyalty. Pulling off, I headed out to my crib in Long Island. I was done for the night and I needed some good rest.

I wake up the next at 6:46. I went to sleep at three this morning but somehow I still managed to wake up early; I guess my body was used to it. I slid my feet into my Versace house shoes and grabbed my Versace robe from the chair that sat near my bed. I went into the restroom to handle my hygiene then went downstairs to cook me something to eat. Because this was the house I didn't trust bitches at, I had to always cook for myself when I stayed. At my other two spots, a bitch naked was how I liked it. Over the stove scrambling eggs and shit.

I pulled out some fully cooked bacon, because a nigga couldn't cook for shit, some eggs and grands biscuits. I hooked it up fast, ate then headed outside to my babies. When I stepped outside, the sun was shining bright. The water currents from the small pond and the birds chirping soothed the moment. That shit made me miss coming home. It was always a peace that a nigga needed. With the way my lifestyle was, peace was always good.

"Rock, China!" I called my male and female Pits and waited for them to get to me. From where I stood, I could see them running towards me. They both jumped up and began playing with me because they hadn't seen me in a while. I rubbed both their heads then commanded for them to sit. I went to the shack to retrieve their food and began making their bowls of Pedigree.

Watching the dogs chow down like they hadn't ate in years, I stood back and watched my surroundings. A nigga had a fat ass crib with everything I needed. I had a pool the size of a fucking lake. I kid you not. Some days, we would ride our jet skis in there and even do donuts. I had a basketball court, a sauna room that sat off the side and a pond. The house itself was so big I had wings like the white house.

Looking around my yard like I did every time I came to this crib I had to wipe a bead of sweat off my forehead. Although I loved this house, this shit was lonely as fuck. It's like reality began to set in. A nigga needed someone to share this shit with. I wanted kids running around and a wife in the kitchen. It's crazy because I constantly bashed women and didn't see myself settling down but hey I guess things changed. Just the thought of things changing, I headed upstairs to begin getting dressed. I needed to see her and I prayed I could stop her before she left for school. I really didn't know what to say. I just prayed I wouldn't be making a fool out of myself.

By the time I got to Morgan's crib, it was a little after 2 pm. I had to practically beg Nana just to tell me where her family stayed. Every time Morgan would come to me, she would be in an uber or I would pick her up from some secret location. The minute I pulled up, I wanted to turn back around. There were so many people outside of the home and because everyone wore a pink shirt with a tree on the front, it was evident that it was a family reunion. I got out the car and walked up to the first person I saw.

"How you doing, ma'am, is Morgan here?"

"Morgan?" she was kind of hesitant. And you are?"

"I'm a friend."

"A friend?"

"Yes. I'm Marcell. Is she here?' I asked growing impatient.

"Give me a second." she looked like she was unsure if she wanted to call her. I took it upon myself to walk all the way in the yard and blend in with the crowd of people. I was the only one without a shirt, so I know I stood out like a sore thumb.

Moments later, Morgan came from in the house. She too was wearing a pink shirt with some duke shorts and pink Nike Huaraches. Even dressed down she was bad. She wore a confused look when she saw me but she came to me.

"Marco, what are you doing here?"

"Oh, I'm Marco now?" I asked because her ass never called me Marco. As much as I hated her calling me Marcell I was now used to it. Even my granny called me Marco but she added the Polo to it just clowning.

"How did you...."

"Don't worry bout all that." I cut her off. "I'm here now so go get yo shit and let's roll out."

"I'm not going nowhere with you. Better yet, you could leave. I don't even know why you're here." As bad as I wanted to curse her ass out I held my composure.

"Look, ma, please don't make this hard for me. I'm trying and trust me I never try. I apologize about what went down last time. I didn't mean for you to see that shit."

"Marcell, you foul as fuck. You just shut me out and then expect for me to just let it go."

"I said I apologize ma. A nigga really mean it. I promise I want shut you out no more. Don't make me beg you because I don't know how to beg." I walked up on her and looked her in her eyes. She lightly stepped back and began looking around the yard. I could tell because her family was here she was kind of reluctant.

"Don't make me cause a scene baby. Just get yo shit. I'll be in the car." I walked off. If she decided to come I would love that shit but if she didn't I would just give up.

No LIE, when my aunt came to get me and said someone was here for me I didn't imagine it was Marcell. I knew it wasn't Nana because she would have said *"that fast tail little girl out there"* but she didn't. She wore a strange look. When I walked out, I was shocked as hell. He was looking good but that didn't change me still being upset with him. The way he showed up and demanded I go with him turned me on though. I was still mad, but guess what? I was in the house grabbing my bag about to leave with him. You damn right. I wasn't about to miss the opportunity of being with him. A part of me wished we could make love under the moon but I failed to mention I was a virgin. I was leaving tomorrow to go back to school so I swept love making under the rug. I can't miss what I never had right?

"Where we going?" I asked the moment I was in the car.

"Don't trip; just roll." he said and got ready to pull off. Right then, Cambree's rental car pulled up and she was eyeing the car being nosey. I slightly leaned back but I knew her mom would tell her it was me. *Owell I'm gone,* I thought.

Driving down the street, I tried my hardest not to look at Marcell. He was looking good as hell in an all-white Gucci short set and some Gucci shades with clear lenses and gold frames. He reminded me so much of Jacquees but taller with a really sexy face. Not saying Jacquees not sexy but Marcell was fire.

"A nigga ain't used to no shit like this ma. I'm really feeling you Morg. It's something about you that's different from the rest of these hoes. It's like you keep a nigga leveled. I push you away because I don't know how to love. All I know is to get money and survive. My lifestyle is hard to deal with but if you ride with me I'll make you a priority." He looked over at me then turned back to the road. My heart melted right there in his leather seat. I was beyond speechless.

"I'm feeling you, too, but I can't do this?" I spoke sadly.

"Why, you got somebody else claiming you?" he asked then got upset. The way he said it kinda scared me. I could tell his ass was jealous no matter how hard he tried to act.

"No, Marcell, I'm leaving to go back to school." He didn't look at me and he remained silent. He nodded his head and now I felt awkward as hell. I mean, what was I supposed to do? I had another two years left before I got my masters and all this time I had been focused.

———

"A skating rink?" I looked over at Marcell. I didn't take him for the type of nigga that enjoyed skating. However, this was the livest skating rink in town and it popped on the weekends. Therefore, I figured he hung out here because it stayed packed with ballers.

"Girl, just get yo ass out." he got out and closed the door. He stood in front of his car and waited for me to get out. Of course I pulled the sun visor down to check my appearance and apply some gloss. It's bad enough I was dressed in this damn family reunion shirt. When I stepped out, he looked annoyed. I brushed past his ass and walked to the entrance. When I got to the door, I pulled out my wallet so that I can pay for myself. I wanted him to know I didn't need anything from him. As a matter of fact, I was gonna pay for his ass too and buy a few drinks.

"Man, what you doing?" he asked again annoyed.

"What it look like?" I ignored him and pulled out the money.

"Marco!" the security stepped up and dapped him up. After talking to the man, he pulled my arm and we entered the rink. I swear it was like time stopped. All eyes were on us and I could hear chatter from all the people inside. I felt very weird so my shy ass hid under his arm.

"Nah, don't get all shy and shit now ma."

"I'm not shy." I smirked.

"Yeah, okay." he said before pulling me towards the skate rentals.

"What size?"

"Seven." he ordered my skates and now I was confused. I know this nigga didn't think I was gonna skate by myself.

"Where yo skates?"

"I don't skate girl."

"Nigga, yo ass skating today. You ain't bout to have me out here alone."

"Nah, I'm good. You go ahead baby. I'mma be right there playing Galaga." he pointed to the vintage arcade machine. I hit him with a side-eye then went to put on my skates. After I was done, I made sure Marco was in eye reach as I made my way to the floor. I waited for the crowd coming around to wind down before I skated out into the crowd. One thing I knew how to do was skate. So in no time I had a nice rhythm and I was grooving to the music.

Yeah, I'm the only young nigga who's poppin' that
Got it jumpin' out the heat there like who coppin' that?
New G Wagon got her braggin', put a lock on that
Niggas always hit her DM, she don't holla back, woo. woo,
copy that

The DJ was playing Meek Mill 'Whatever You Need' so I was

rapping to the lyrics. Every time I went around, I smiled and stuck my tongue out at Marcell. I noticed every time I went around there was a different person in his face. However, he was focused on me and what I was doing on the floor. A few more rounds around I was ready to go keep him occupied but I noticed a chocolate girl in his face along with some other chick. The way he was smiling was like he was happily entertained. Instead of leaving the floor, I kept skating. As much as it hurt me, I didn't want to look like a hater so I let him do him; I just wish he would have left me where I was at so he could.

The DJ switched the song to Lil Durks 'India' and now I was really in my feelings. When I went around, Marcell and I locked eyes. I rolled my eyes on the sly trying not to show my jealousy but I'm sure he caught it. I kept skating and minding my business. This was my last night in New York so I wasn't gonna let him ruin it.

Skating and minding my business, I avoided looking in the direction were Marcell was last standing. Out of nowhere, I felt a pair of arms wrap around my waist. I would have pulled back but the smell of his Burberry cologne let me know it was him.

I can't lie, I can't tell my guys
That I'm in love and I feel so shy
And we both turnt up we from the Chi
But I don't ask about her other guy

Marcell rapped the lyrics to the song causing goosebumps up my back and arms.

"Stop tripping ma. These hoes don't mean shit to me. And after tonight you my bitch and I belong to you." Once again I melted.

"So if you belong to me then stay out these hoes' face." I pushed up off him nearly causing him to fall. He thought his ass was slick using me as leverage. When I turned around I couldn't do shit but laugh. For the first time, his ass was stuck; Literally. He was stuck holding the wall and he looked like he wasn't moving no time soon. I laughed as I made a few rounds around him.

"You think this shit funny!" he yelled as I went around again. I was literally in tears laughing. When I looked back, he had come up out his skates and was now walking across the floor mad. I was still laughing as I made my way up the ramp.

"Awe, baby, can't skate." I teased him.

"Man, that shit ain't funny girl. And hell nah I can't skate with yo big head ass."

"I'm sorry, baby, gimme kiss." I was laughing again walking over to him with my arms extended.

"Payback's a bitch." he nudged the top of my head. We both laughed.

"Aye, Boss, we got a group of niggas outside fighting." one of the security guards walked up. I was now confused as to why security was coming for him.

"Watch my shawty." he told security and walked out the door without saying a word.

"Watch me? Oh, hell nah. I gotta go with him."

"Ma'am, he wants you to stay right here."

"I ain't staying"....I was about to say until I heard shots ring out from outside. I looked at security and we both ran towards the front. Before I could make it to the door, Marcell was coming back in and grabbed my arm.

"You know what to do." he told the security and he nodded. Marcell and I quickly exited and headed for the car. In my head, I was thanking God I had on sneakers because he was walking fast and pulling me right along. When we got to the car we hopped in and sped off. I wanted so bad to ask him what went down but I didn't want him tripping on me.

"What a way to start a first date." he joked to lighten the mood.

"I'm just glad you're okay." I told him truthfully.

"I'mma always be okay baby. Trust me." his cocky ass said then turned up the music. *Damn he sexy.*

WHEN MORGAN and I pulled up to my crib, her nosey ass was looking at the crib in awe. It was big as fuck but I also knew what she was thinking. *'I've never brought her here.'* Morgan been to a couple of my cribs but this house was the one she's never been to. This was the house that held so much sentimental value because my granny left it to me when she received my mom's insurance from her death. The crib wasn't as big when I received it but with a few adjustments I made this muthafucka look like something out of a magazine.

This was the home where my dogs lived and the home I wanted to raise my family. Morgan leaving tomorrow was about to change. Little did she know, her ass was gonna give a nigga a few babies and sit right here and wait on daddy to come home. Tonight I was gonna do everything to show her I needed her in my life. I don't know what it is about her ass but she was gonna rock my last name and no other bitch could stand in the way of it.

Tonight at the rink her ass was tripping which annoyed me because I was there with her. This little skeeza came and hollered at me but it wasn't nothing too serious. When I saw her pouting, I did the unthinkable. I put on a pair of skates for the first time and went to my baby. This how I know she the one. I wouldn't skate for no damn body. I didn't give a fuck if I was the owner; you couldn't get me out on that rink for shit.

"Who's house?" I knew she was gonna ask.

"It's ours Morg."

"Ours?" she asked confused.

"Yes, this where you bout to live. This our castle princess. Now bring yo big head ass on," I smiled and opened the door.

"Hopefully, I ain't gotta share it with nobody." she said slickly. I knew she meant with another bitch. As bad as I wanted to feed into her games I chose not to.

"Man, gone with that shit. The only people we gonna share it with is our kids."

"Kids? Nigga, I ain't having no kids."

"You saying that now. After I put this dick deep up in you, you gone wanna bless a nigga with ten rugrats." I spoke into her ear as I rubbed my hand down her backside.

"Yeah okay." she rolled her eyes and stepped up out my fundals.

"Follow me." I told her as she continued to examine my crib.

When we made it to my bedroom, I wasted no time hopping in the shower and sliding into some ball shorts. I was determined to fuck the dawg shit out her tonight because I was trying to make her stay. I understood the value of knowledge but when you had a nigga that was rich, and willing to hand you a business, there was need to over work. Morgan didn't know what I had planned for her but if she decided to stay I was gonna give her the world.

About an hour later, Morgan entered my room fresh from the shower wearing one of my t-shirts. She laid down beside me and I could tell she was nervous for some odd reason.

"Did you enjoy yourself tonight?" I asked her.

"Yes I had a cool time. But what happened outside?"

"Some bullshit. Nothing major. Make a long story short ma, niggas was outside tripping and I had to send a message. One thing, I don't play bout my business. I didn't kill nobody like I wanted to but I had to send a message."

"Oh." was all she said. "What made you want to open a skating rink?"

"Really, because there's none in our city. I wanted somewhere the kids could enjoy them self."

"Awww, that's so dope."

"Good looking."

"So what is it you're going to school for?"

"To become a teacher. I love kids. I'd rather work with elementary school kids though."

"That's what's up. So what do you plan on doing?"

"Well, right now I want to start off at a daycare or like a center for kids."

"You ever think about opening your own?"

"Yessss." she beamed. I could tell she enjoyed the thought of, not only the kids but opening up her own business. *Perfect.*

"Once I work for a few years and save I'll open up something. I mean I could get the money from my parents but I'd rather do it on my own."

"Now that's dope as fuck." I told her smiling. Little did she know I already had plans for her. Especially now that I knew what she wanted to do.

"Tell me about yourself Marcell." she asked. Morgan and I had talked so many times about so many different things but for the first time we were finally getting to know each other. I'm sure it had a lot to do with me making us official. On other occasions, Morgan steered clear from these conversations.

"Ain't much to tell ma. I sale dope, own a skating rink and fuck bitches."

"Marcell!" she whined.

"Well you asked."

"When am I gonna meet your *G Moms*?" she asked mocking me.

"When you become my wife."

"Damn, I gotta be your wife to meet her?"

"Yeah ma. Everybody don't meet her Morg. I gotta know you really wit a nigga."

"I am really wit you." she said and dropped her head. I could tell something was really bothering her but she was holding back.

"Why every time something on your mind you put your head down. Let me know what's up."

"It's really nothing. I mean, other than me leaving tomorrow." she sounded sad. "Can you wait for me?" she asked and I didn't know what to say. I've never waited for a chick, shit. I didn't know if I had it in me.

"Look ma. I'm feeling you and you're feeling me. You leaving ain't sitting too well with me."

"Okay, but are we official?"

"Yeah."

"Well if I'm your girl how could you not wait for me? If the shoe was on the other foot, you'll want me to wait for you."

"True, but I'm a man ma. We don't wait." I could tell that last statement hurt her so I tried to adjust my words and make her feel better.

"I'll try ma." I kissed her forehead.

"Promise," her eyes pleaded.

"Promise." I assured her. Next thing I know we were in a full blown make-out session. Shit got so hot so fast, I slid the shirt she was wearing over her head. I looked down at her plump melons and they sat so perfectly. Her nipples were rock hard but once again she looked nervous.

"Relax baby." I told her and laid her down. I planted kisses down her neck to her belly button and her moans alone was making my dick harder. As bad as I wanted to taste her, I couldn't do it. A nigga like me wasn't eating no pussy. It wasn't that I thought she was dirty or nothing but hanging with a bitch like Nana, wasn't no telling who been inside of her.

"Marcell." she whispered. I gave her my attention in response. "Please don't hurt me." I didn't know what that meant but it held sincerity. Now, her heart I could promise not to hurt but this pussy, I was about to kill it like *Saw* 7.

Because Morgan wasn't wearing panties, it gave me all the access I needed. I slid my b-ball shorts down then slid a finger into her pussy. Her shit was tighter than I expected but of course that came from the hot shower she had just taken. After fingering her for some time, I stood up so I could adjust her body to my likings. I pulled her all the way to the edge of the bed. Because my bed sat up high I was able to adjust myself right at her pretty golden pussy. I could see her eyeing my dick and damn she looked scared. I quickly took my position and eased it into her hole. Well at least I tried because she was too damn tight. It was crazy because her pussy was dripping wet but a nigga couldn't get in.

"Morgan. You a virgin?" I asked looking into her eyes. She gave me a look of embarrassment but there was no reason to be. Instead of responding, tears started pouring from her eyes and that let me know right there, her ass was a virgin indeed.

Just the thought made me hurry up and slide in. From the way she was flinching I knew it hurt her but I needed her in the worst way.

"Ahhh." she screamed out.

"It's gonna only hurt for a moment baby." I whispered in her ear. I was now laying on top of her because I needed to ease my way in. Once I was all the way in, I began slow stroking her to get her used to my girth. Tears was still pouring from her eyes and I hated that shit. Lil baby was making a nigga soft for her.

"After today, ma, you belong to me. I need your mind, body and soul. Okay?" I asked with every stroke. When she didn't answer me, I began to punish her.

"You hear me Princess?" I started stroking faster and harder.

"Ye..yes...YES! Baby, I hear you." she cried out. I bit down on my bottom lip and already I was ready to bust. But fuck that I wasn't going out like that. I pulled out of her and quickly kissed her neck. I gave myself some time then I slid back into her.

"Morgan, you belong to me ma. You can't just leave a nigga now baby. You can't give me this good pussy then leave ma." I was all in my feelings. Fuck no, I refused to let her leave me. This pussy was too damn good.

"Ooooh, Marcell. Oooh, shit! I think I'm peeing!" she screamed out.

"Nah, that ain't pee. Daddy just making you squirt. Let that shit out."

"Oh my goddddddddd!" again she screamed out.

"Let it out baby." I lifted off the bed and now had her legs spread wide. I was hitting it raw dog and I was gonna let all my seeds fill her up. I was gonna get her pregnant one way or another and I didn't give a fuck. She wasn't leaving me.

"Marcell! Oh my god I love you!." she blurted out. As good as her pussy felt, I wanted to reply with an *I love you* but I couldn't. I had to know this shit was real and not just because the dick was good.

For the next hour, I fucked Morgan until she busted at least three more nuts. Finally done, I dropped my load off in her and laid on top of her for a while so every drip of my cum could fall into her warm pussy.

"Marcell." she called my name out in fear.

"Sup ma?"

"Did you nut in me?" she asked a stupid ass question.

"Do it matter?"

"Oh, my god. You have to take me to Walgreen's." She lifted up pushing me off her.

"Walgreens? For what?"

"I have to get a plan b."

"You got me fucked up. Sit yo stupid ass down man."

"What do you mean? What if I get pregnant?"

"And?" I asked annoyed. "You act like this was a mistake. Oh, you love me when the dick in you but you don't love me enough to give me a baby?"

"I can't have no kids right now," she said it like she meant it so I called it like I seen it. I lifted up and headed for the bathroom to wash up. I shot over my shoulder.

"Don't trip; let me wash my dick. I'mma take you to get yo pill but I'mma tell you this, when the next bitch running around with my seed I bet not hear shit." I told her and slammed the door. Although I didn't expect to ever have kids, I just wanted her to feel how I felt at the moment. Lil mama had just crushed a nigga and fucked up my whole mood. She could leave for all I gave a fuck. I was gonna drop her off and never bother to call her ass again.

Fuck her.

"WHERE IS SHE CAMBREE?" my mother asked a million times.

"I don't know; she's not answering."

"Well, you better find her ass. She has school tomorrow and I know her ass ain't on that damn plane because all her shit here."

"Mom, you're the one who let the guy pick her up."

"I didn't know she was leaving."

"I'll find her." I told my mother because she was bugging. She wanted me to find Morgan but the only info she could give me was the guy was young, had on expensive jewelry and drove an exotic car. There was a million niggas in NY that fit the description, however it only meant one thing; he was a dope boy.

Morgan's ass was about to hear my mouth, something she hated but her ass was in violation. Whatever little nigga had her about to miss her flight had her open. She always had a passion for dboys but this wasn't like her. She was a straight A student and her education was a passion. I knew deep down that it wasn't nobody but Nana hoe ass that had her in these streets meeting niggas. I couldn't stand that little bitch and this was one of the reasons. I mean, we all had our share of a hood nigga but Nana fucked the whole New York and was a very bad influence. I dialed Nana's number and waited for her to answer.

"Hello."

"Where Morgan?"

"Hi to you too." she sassed.

"Look, I ain't got time for your shit little girl; where is my little cousin? She's about to miss her flight back home."

"I don't know where she at." I went to hang up but I could hear her screaming through the phone.

"How long she been gone? Did you see who she left with?" her nosey ass asked question after question.

"If she ain't with you why do it mat...." before I could finish, Morgan was walking through the door. I hung up on Nana and walked over to her.

"Where the fuck have you been? and who is this nigga you riding around with?" I asked angry.

"A friend." she said through a bloodshot red pair of eyes. I could clearly tell she wasn't high, however it looked like she had been crying. Before I could interrogate, my mother came into the room lashing out.

"Where the hell yo fast ass been?"

"I was out aunty." she spoke as if she didn't want to be bothered.

"Out? You got your got damn nerves. Your mother been calling like crazy. You ain't gonna take me to an early grave. Go pack yo shit so your cousin could take you to the airport. Bout to miss your flight and shit chasing these got damn boys." my mother stormed off. My mom was used to the many thugs I've dated but after what happened with Major and I, she hated thugs and forbade me to date another.

Morgan didn't even bother to put up a fight. It was something about the look in her eyes that was all too familiar. Whoever this nigga was, she was in love with, and it was me all over again.

Morgan had finally come down right when I was done feeding

Camiya and Lil Cameron. She looked so worn out I didn't bother to say a word. I cleaned up the mess they had made and went to tell my mother I be back. I grabbed the kids' backpacks and we headed out the door. Once we were in the car, I pulled off heading to the airport. As we drove, Morgan hadn't said two words. This wasn't like her because she hadn't even played with the kids. I turned my music down and looked over at her. She was staring out the window and didn't bother to blink.

"Whoever this little nigga got you bugging Morg, ain't worth you missing out on your education. Now, I'm not trying to preach. I just want you to understand I've been in your shoes. I don't know the situation with you and him but if he's a street nigga then trust me I've been there." She didn't say a word but I did get her to finally look at me so I continued.

"When I met Major, he was fresh from a break-up. He was the best and most perfect gentleman. I fell in love with that man but guess what, he was in love with someone else. I'm not gonna go all into details but that shit comes with the streets. Now if you don't mind, what happen?" I asked because I couldn't give her encouraging words if I didn't know the case. She looked at me and I could tell she was hesitant. I still looked at Morg as the cute little girl who wore two pigtails that always wanted ice cream. However, I had to understand she wasn't a kid anymore. I never wanted to run her life; I just wanted the best for her.

"I met a guy and he's really nice. Last night we had a big fight because he doesn't want me to leave him for school." she looked back out the window.

"If he loves you he'll make a way. Better yet, he should wait for you. You're on a positive path and he should support you one hundred percent. Let me ask you this and please don't lie." I gave her a look that told her she could confide in me.

"Have you gave him the cookie?" the minute I said it she bust out laughing.

"The cookie?" she burst into laughter. "Cam, I am not seven anymore."

"I know. That's why I'm having this conversation with you."

"Well, if you must know. Yes, last night was my first time."

"I want some cookies mommy." Camiya asked from the backseat. I shot Morgan a look and we both burst out in laughter.

"See." I shook my head looking over at Morg. "So how was it?" I asked because I wanted her to get comfortable when talking about sex.

"It was magical." her eyes beamed. "But it's over now so I guess it doesn't matter."

"So you don't think if he gave a fuck he would have been here stopping you from leaving?"

"That's the thing. He tried but I couldn't miss school." she said but I knew it was more to it.

"I hate that you had to give him the cookie and now it ends like this. I hope you take it as a lesson learned. Find you a good guy. A doctor or shit even a basketball player. These street niggas ain't shit ma." I told her just as we were pulling up to the departure.

"Please don't tell on me." she said with pleading eyes.

"I won't. I promise." I gave her a reassuring smile. I wanted Morgan to trust me. I needed her to know she could talk to me about anything.

"I'll call you when I land." She kissed me on the cheek then reached back and kissed the kids. She was smiling again but I knew once she was on that plane, her smile would be washed away.

———

After so much begging, I agreed to take the kids to the arcade that was located inside of the mall. I was gonna get Lil Cameron a few pair of shoes because his mother was coming to pick him up in the morning. I didn't get to spend much time with my nephew so every chance I got I'd pick him up, take him out and make sure we go shopping.

Cameron had just turned four and him and Camiya were besties. Because he and Camiya were so close in age, they loved each other and were more like sister and brother. Although I didn't care for Kaliyah, Lil Cameron was my baby. I mean, she was cool or whatever but she tried too hard to fit in. She had my brother's baby and I mean damn that was enough. She constantly acted like she was his girl but he didn't want any parts of her. She was really a bug-a-boo. I lived all the way in Miami now and she would call everyday just to gossip. I was never the type to have friends and I mean what could we possibly talk about with us being miles away.

"Mommy, gimme some quarters." Camiya asked eagerly.

"I want quarters too TiTi." Lil Cameron asked as they ran towards the arcade. I swear he looked so much like Camiere it made me miss him so much. Camiere had chosen to name him after our brother Cameron that had been killed. Truthfully, I dreaded calling him Cameron but it did make me feel close to my now deceased brother. I missed both my brothers like crazy. Without them, I felt so alone in this world. They are my everything and thanks to the man that broke my heart, my brother was now in jail on a life sentence.

Camiere had been framed by Boss Major which is Camiya's father. When he broke my heart, I left to live in Miami and never told nobody I was having Major's baby. Not my brother nor Major. I didn't want people to think I was doing it because I wanted to trap him so instead I left the city. I came down to spend time with my mother who I missed dearly and in the next couple months I was on a flight back home. As much as I missed New York, there were too many memories here. I lost two brothers, along with my dignity and broken heart. The one man I would have never thought would break me down, tormented me like I wasn't shit. He promised me his heart but it belonged to someone else. Him and his wife made a mockery out of not only me but my brother as well.

I know I'm supposed to hate Major, but a part of me still craved him. I always asked myself *what if*. That man was the true definition of a Boss. Everything about him was perfect and in my heart I believe if it wasn't for Yanese, we would be happily married with a house full of kids. I would have given him four more babies. There wasn't a flaw in him except his ex who he never stopped loving. He treated me so good that my expectations of a man were high. If I couldn't find a man like Boss then I didn't want no parts of him. And that's why I was still single until this day.

Looking down at the tattoo that read *Boss* on my hand brought back memories. There was a crown on the *B* and the rest was in fine cursive. All these years later and I had never covered the tattoo up. And that's how I knew, I would always be in love with him. *Bitter Sweet*.

"Maybe, it's not his Yanese. Your over reacting ma."

"Dajah, I'm not. That baby looked just like his ass. And from my calculations, it's about right. She looked like she was at least five."

"How you know she didn't meet a nigga as soon as she left town?"

"She looked just like Blessin!" I burst out into tears. This shit was killing me. I knew my eyes weren't deceiving me. It had been so long since I'd seen her but she looked exactly the same. Nothing had changed except she had gotten a little thicker. Of course it was probably baby fat.

When I looked at the little girl that had run up to her, I was stopped in my tracks. The little girl looked like a split image of my daughter. I know the baby had to be conceived when they were together but the thought of him having another child by another woman bothered me.

"So are you gonna tell him?" Dajah asked bringing me from my thoughts.

"No. Hell NO."

"Yanese, you have to tell him."

"I'll think about it." I told her then informed her I would call her back. I couldn't think straight. Telling Major was not an option. I knew Major loved me and yes I did trust him, but I was no fool. *A baby?* All he would do is reach out to her then they would began to bond. There was already enough shit going on with Major and Camiere so there was no telling what Cambree was up too.

After the whole incident at my parents' home, we later learned that Camiere had actually survived the shooting. The whole thing with Major setting him up was a puzzle to me, however I had to ride with my husband. Camiere wasn't to be trusted and with the power he possessed I knew he could make shit happen from in jail. I was actually shocked nothing has went down since his incarceration. A part of me felt that's why Cambree had resurfaced so I was gonna keep my mouth shut and hopefully the bitch goes back to the island she came from.

Smack!

I dropped the plate that was in my hand and it hit the ground breaking into a million pieces.

"Boy, you scared me." I lied then hurried off to get the broom so I could clean up the mess. Major had caught me off guard and slapped me on my ass that was now stinging. I was stuck in one spot still in a daze which is why I used the excuse of him scaring me. When I came back with the broom, I hoped like hell he would disappear into the house but nah that nigga was right there waiting.

"What's up ma? You good?" he asked as if he could tell I was crying.

"Yes, I'm fine."

"Yeah, aight." he said as if he knew I was lying.

"I'm good, Major, stop looking at me like that." He was eyeing me and I was sure the hurt was written all over my face.

I tried to hide the pain as much as I could. So I busied myself sweeping up the glass. I was also trying so hard to keep my hands from shaking. Major stood back and crossed his arm over the other. I would be a lie if I said this man wasn't sexy as hell but right now I didn't know how to feel about him. I mean, I didn't have the proof that the baby was his but there were too many similarities. The other child she had with her, I was sure it wasn't Majors. It was something about that little girl that trained my eyes onto her.

I wonder if he knows about the baby and just never told me? Oh, my God, what if he still messes with her? What if he has her stashed away? So many thoughts were going through my mind I had to get away him.

"I'm... umm... I'm gonna meet Candy at the shop bae." I spoke to Major without any eye contact.

"Aight, ma. I'mma go up in my office and get some work done. What's for dinner?"

"Well, since it's just us, Ill grab us something on my way back."

"Okay." He kissed my neck and headed upstairs. I went into my room, grabbed my purse and I was out the door.

———

Pulling up to Candy's nail shop, I parked out back then headed in through the back exit. When I walked in, there was a shop full of people seated and people waiting to be seen. There was 25 nail techs from Korean to Blacks. One thing we didn't do was discriminate. There was enough room for everyone to eat. Though I had given the nail shop to Candy, I still had money tied in it, but I let her do her. I had to give it to her, she was running her shit smoothly. She had the most talked about nail salon and you could even get waxed and massaged.

As I walked through, everyone greeted me then Coco informed me I could find Candy in the back. The last time I saw her was the night she came over after her and Trig had a fight over his baby mama. I knew we had some catching up to do, and I couldn't wait to drop this bomb on her. When I found her, she was talking to a nail tech. I stood to the side and let her handle her business. Moments later, she finally looked up and a smile graced her face. I swear, this was my girl. Now, don't get me wrong, Dajah was still my bestie but me and Candy had grown close.

Since Major and I fell back a little from the game, Jigga and Dajah had got them a few businesses and they too were enjoying life. Boo was still doing Boo. He was still single and a asshole. But that's still my dog. Dajah now had one more child and all she did was work, cook and clean. We rarely saw much of each other but she would always be my bestie.

"Montana!!!" Candy yelled causing me to laugh. Every time I heard that name, all I could do was laugh.

"Heyyyy, Boo!" We exchanged hugs.

"What yo ass got going on?"

"Girl too much. Let's go in my office." she said and pulled my arm towards the room.

"What's up? I know something wrong because of the way you said it."

"Girllll... I'm just going through it with this bitch Jasmyn. She's really a pain in my ass. Shit is hectic in the streets; this whole shit with Cap still fucking with me and shit bout to get real with these pigs." she sighed.

"This the reason I wanted you out the game ma. I told you raise your child and enjoy life."

"I wish it was that easy."

"So what's up with Jasmyn; do we gotta ride on this hoe or what?" I asked because she knew I would still get dirty. I knew exactly how she felt because I once dealt with a looney baby mama. Only problem was, my baby mama so money hungry we paid the bitch to leave the state. Now the difference with Jasmyn is, she's in love with Trig so paying her off wasn't an option.

"I got a feeling he's still fucking her. She plays on my phone and I try not to go there because that's his baby mama but sooner or later I'mma go there with the hoe."

"So if he is fucking her, what you gonna do?" I searched her face for the truth. She looked so worn out I could tell she was tired.

"I'mma leave." She dropped her head. The room got quiet and I didn't know what to say. I knew Candy loved Trig but what's love got to do with it. I'm living proof.

"Before you jump the gun, get facts. Don't just let this hating ass hoe fuck up what y'all got." I told her then I became sad again. Candy had so much going on, I didn't want to bring my burdens on her so I decided to let the baby thing go for now. I was gonna do my own investigation and, when I found out the truth, I don't know what I would do from there.

Sigh.

"I OBJECT!" The attorney shouted at the DA frustrated.

"Sustained."

"I'm sorry, but he is a threat to the streets. He's a known drug dealer and very harmful to our community."

"Objection! My client is here on a murder charge. No one has come forward and said my client sales drugs."

"Mr. Pitman, what are the new discoveries found?" The judge looked over the rim of his specks.

"Well, we have a tape of my clients whereabouts the night and time the victim was pronounced dead. Your Honor, this is the same tape that magically disappeared from the evidence room."

"Are you ready to present the tape?"

"Yes sir."

"Bailiff." The Judge nodded to the bailiff for him to play the tape. When the lights went off the tape began to play and the courtroom watched the 30 minutes of footage in silence.

After the tape went off, everyone was applauding.

"We have DNA for Christ's sake!" The DA shouted.

"Yes, DNA that's inconclusive, Your Honor. My clients DNA is nowhere on the evidence." the lawyer spoke with confidence.

I reached over and whispered to the DA. The moment the last word left my mouth, he was screaming down my throat.

"Whose side are you on for Christ's sake?!" the DA looked over at me angry.

"May I, Your Honor?" he nodded for me to proceed.

"I'm sorry but I'm not in the job of having innocent people locked away. The evidence are not enough to keep the defendant in jail another day longer. Now had this case been given to me when it first happened it wouldn't have went this far." The judge looked down at his watch then back to the courtroom.

"This matter will be continued for two weeks from today. Now Mr. Guzman if you have any more evidence that can keep the defendant locked away present them. If not I'm going to throw this case out." The judge stood to his feet and nodded his head at me and Andrew. I stood to my feet and then looked over at his sexy ass. He wore a smirk on his face that made my pussy jump in my pants suit. The bailiff escorted him out the courtroom and I walked away with pure confidence. We had this case on lock and soon he would be home and in my bed giving me that good dick.

━━━

Sitting at the bar of a local restaurant, I threw back shot after shot. Thoughts of him invaded my mind and I was ready for this shit to be over. Being a cop was hard and appearing in court was even worse. That shit took so much energy out of me sometimes I wished I still worked as a CO in the prison.

After the last shot, I think I had about enough. I pulled out my money and laid it on the bar. I went to stand up and nearly tripped.

"Wooo, shit, ma you too damn sexy to be falling. A nigga like me gonna be laughing." I turned around and was met with a man that was so sexy I was lost for words. His muscular frame stood in my way and he still held onto my arm. It was something about him that looked so familiar but as tipsy as I was I didn't have time to think.

"That's rude." I giggled.

"I'm just saying. I'mma ask are you okay first, then I'm laughing."

"Well, thanks to you I didn't fall." I flirted.

"So now you owe me." he smirked.

"Is that so? Well ,let me buy you a drink."

"That would be nice." he took a seat. "I would ask to join you but it looks like you can't hang anymore."

"I'm a big girl, trust me, I got this." I looked at the bartender and nodded for him to give me two shots of Remy VSOP.

"I'm Bee by the way." he extended his hand.

"I'm Veronica."

"Nice to meet yo sexy ass Veronica.

After talking to Bee for a while, I had to admit he was fine as hell with a great personality. We laughed, joked and flirted back and forth. By the time I looked at my watch, it was nearly midnight. I knew Melvin was gonna talk shit but right now I didn't care.

"Let me take you home ma. You a little too drunk to drive."

"You're not gonna kill me or rape me are you?"

"The only thing I'll kill is that pussy. Now as far as rape, do it look like I'm the type of guy to have to take pussy?" We both laughed. He wasn't lying. He was so fine I knew women threw themselves at him constantly.

"Okay, Bee." I stood up and grabbed my purse. I was so drunk he had to practically carry me out the restaurant.

Brent

"Sssss! Yes baby. Fuck this pussy daddy!"

"You like that shit?"

"Ohhh yes! It's sooo big! Ughhhh it's sooooo.....!"

"You a big girl right?"

"Ooooh, yesss, I'm a big girl." she cried out.

I had Veronica ass on all four beating her pussy up like Martin on that one boxing match episode. I ain't gone lie, I didn't expect this bitch pussy to be this fucking good. Her shit was so wet she caused a puddle underneath the both of us.

"This some good ass pussy ma." I was damn near about to cum. I pulled out and demanded she turned over.

"Let me find out you bout to tap out?" she began talking shit.

"I'm in this pussy for the whole night." I moaned out as I eased my way back inside her. Our lips touched and she pulled my bottom lip into her mouth. She began sucking on my lip and that shit was making me hit it harder. I've never really been the kissing type but the heat of the moment was so perfect anything went. Now, I've had some good pussy in my days but this bitch pussy was made of gold. I don't know what Boss was thinking when he shitted on her. With every stroke, her shit gripped my dick damn near strangling me.

"I'm cumming...oh my God, it's coming!" she began to pant. The way her body moved I could tell she wanted me to pound her guts out so I did just that. I started hitting it so hard I felt myself banging against something inside of her. Next thing I know, her juices oozed down my dick and that shit felt too good. Not being able to hold it in, I released behind her. I let every last drop of my nut spill into the condom before I rolled off of her. We both laid there breathing hard.

After moments of silence I heard light snoring that made me look over at her. Her ass was knocked out already. I laughed not only because she was knocked out but because this shit was too damn easy. I lifted from the bed and went to dispose the condom. I took a quick shower then headed back in the room to grab my phone.

Me: *shit was easy son!*
    Marco: *ha haha you a fool*
    Me: *bitch got some fire ass pussy*
    Marco: *you wild B!*
    Me: *just wanted to touch bases. One*
    Marco: *one!*

Right when I was done texting Marc another text came through.

Mercedes: *I know yo punk ass see me calling*
    Me: *man I been busy*
    Mercedes: *yeah I bet. Which bitch in yo bed now?*
    Me: *man don't start. Nigga been running all day. I'm tired and I'm going to bed*

The minute I sat the phone down it started ringing. I shook my head because I already knew it was Mercedes now calling. I let that shit vibrate and I climbed back in the bed and pulled Veronica next to me. I wanted to wake her up for another round but I chose to let her be. *I'mma beat that shit up in the morning,* I thought before I drifted to sleep.

—

The next morning, I was woken up to Veronica on the phone screaming.

"I've been working! This is a long case Mel. I'll be leaving soon." were her last words and she disconnected the line. She quickly began to get dressed. She was wearing a towel so that told me she had showered. A nigga must have been knocked out because I didn't hear shit.

"Good morning, I'm sorry. I didn't mean to wake up."

"You good. But what's up, though, you straight?"

"Yes. my husband been calling all night. I have to go."

"Husband? Damn, ma." I chuckled.

"Yeah, I mean it's pretty complicated."

"I understand. So when can I see you again?" I asked. She stopped mid-stride of buttoning her shirt and looked over at me.

"Umm. I don't know. Between my job and my husband I be pretty busy."

"Damn, so you give me that good pussy and just shake like that?" I chuckled again. No lie baby had a nigga ego crushed. I thought after I put this fire dick on her she would be begging for my attention.

"It's not like that." she sat down on the bed and slid into her pumps. "I'mma see you soon. Let me put my number in your phone." I reached over and grabbed my phone from the nightstand. She entered her number and handed it back. What she did next fucked me up. Bitch leaned down, kissed my forehead, then grabbed her shit. Before she was all the way out the door, I called out to her.

"I gotta see you again." I said sounding like a straight bitch. She smiled and nodded her head. When she vanished I laid back on the bed with so much on my mind. Veronica blew a nigga mind without effort. This shit was strictly business but something told me it was gonna be more. To get her off my mind, I called this little chick Stacy. I was gonna have her come through and cook me some breakfast. I had to go meet with the team later so for the rest of the day I was gonna chill.

"FEDERAL *and local police agencies confiscated over 5,000,000 dollars in cocaine off of a ship that was heading for New York Harbor. Multiple firearms, cocaine and heroin were all discovered on the ship. Early this summer the authorities stumbled upon what seemed to be suspicious activities on the ship that came in and out of Columbia nearly every two weeks. At this moment, we have several men arrested and this case is far from over. U.S. Attorney Michael Kennedy minced no words in describing the individuals who were arrested. In all, sixteen people were taken into custody to face charges for their role in the drug ring.*"

I didn't even let the bitch finish. I slammed my phone into the television so hard it shattered and caused a nice size hole in the middle of the screen. A nigga was beyond pissed off. I took a seat on the couch and dropped my head into my hands. Not only did I lose out on over a million dollars, I also knew that we would have to let shit die down before trying to cop again. Shit was getting crazy fast and I had a feeling it had something to do with when Cap got cracked with them bricks.

Ring

My home phone began ringing off the hook. I ignored every call because a nigga was sick.

"Trayon!" Candy was standing in front of me screaming my name.

"They got the ship," I spoke almost in a whisper. I shook my head then looked up at her to see her reaction but instead she dropped her head and took a seat beside me. For a brief moment, the room fell silent.

"You think this got something to do with....." Before she could finish I cut her off.

"Yep. I really do. Shit been running smooth until that shit happened."

"Also do you think it's ol girl?"

"That I don't know but because the bitch in on it I'mma put her at fault. Brent handled that shit already." I informed her that the plan was in motion.

Knock, Knock, Knock!

Someone was bamming on my door like they lost they mind. Me and Candy looked at each other with slight worry. I don't know why but the first thing came to my mind was the FEDS. I got up from the couch and walked to the door. Looking out the peephole, I shook my head. All hell was about to break loose. I swung the door open and this bitch was standing here with my daughter in her arms looking like she was ready to pop off.

"Not right now, Jas. It's not the right time."

"Oh, it's always the right time. Get yo fucking daughter because I got shit to do. You sitting over here playing house with this hoe well guess what? Yo daughter bout to play with y'all." Before I knew it,

Candy had ran up and swung on Jas knocking her into the door. I had to quickly grab Jay out her arms because she damn near hit her head on the door. Jas didn't get a chance to swing back. Candy was on top of her beating her ass. As bad as I wanted to let it go down, Jayla began screaming so I had to stop it.

"That's enough Candy!"

"Fuck this bitch." I shot breathing hard but still holding Jas down.

"Candy that's enough!" I snatched her back.

"So you let this bitch jump on me with my daughter in my arms? Watch, nigga, you got yours coming." Jas was crying. She snatched Jayla up and whipped the snot running from her nose.

"You better learn how to control this hoe! Next time bitch won't be getting up," Candy shot and stormed off towards the back of the house.

"Man, get from over here, Jas. You gone fuck around and have this girl kill you."

"And you gone let her huh?" Jas asked with so much hatred. A part of me felt bad but she deserved everything she got. She needed to know her place. True, I was the one to blame but that didn't mean she needed to disrespect Candy. This house belonged to Candy so I couldn't be mad at how Candy acted.

"You ain't gon never see my baby." Jas stormed off. Normally, when the bitch threatened me with my baby, I would suck pussy and kiss ass. But not today. I had way bigger things to worry about. Jayla wasn't going nowhere and I would kill Jas if she even tried to take my baby.

"Nigga, I been calling you 90 going north. Why the fucking you looking like that? And why the fuck blood at the doorway?" Marco walked in asking question after question.

"My phone broke and Candy beat the shit out of Jas." I spoke nonchalantly.

"Whatttt?!" he yelled out excited. "Sis beat that hoe ass. Where sis at?"

"Man, that shit ain't cool nigga. Now I gotta deal with them bickering back and forth."

"Come on, my nigga. I mean, it was about time. See, that's your problem, you be letting yo bm get away with too much shit. Sis done put hands on her and now you in yo feelings." he spoke taking a seat. "Wish I was here to see it." he laughed like it was funny.

"Nigga we just lost over a million fucking dollars; that girl shit is the last thing on my mind."

"That's why you in here lookin bitter? Look, my nigga, we gotta take a loss sometimes. That shit didn't even put a dent in our pocket. Now what I'm worried about is them muthafuckas telling and sending them our way. They ain't gonna give they boy up but believe they will roll over on us."

"We gotta figure this shit out. This shit not only about to have us hot but we gotta figure out how the fuck we gone get some more work."

"Yeah, I feel you. We gon get it." he spoke like he had shit under control. That's what I liked about Marco; he didn't let shit bother him. He lived for day to day and didn't care about shit.

"The money gon come but right now, I'm ready to paint the city red. Starting with that bitch and her partner." He lit the blunt that was in his hand and took a long, hard puff. Something was up with this nigga and it wasn't the work we had lost.

"What's up with you nigga?' I asked getting off subject. This nigga was wild and ready to kill cops and shit.

"Bitch got my head fucked up so I'mma take it out on the crackers." He shook his head and took another puff.

"What! Mr. Marco The Don let a bitch get to him?"

"Man, she different. I'm really feeling this bitch. Peep though, I fucked her so I could trap her and keep her around and guess what the bitch do?"

"Trap her?" I asked falling out laughing.

"Man, fuck you. And hell yeah I tried to trap her."

"What she do?" I asked. I had to hear this shit. This wasn't like Marco to want to trap a woman. Kids were the last thing on his mind.

"Bitch took a plan b." Again, I fell out laughing because this nigga was serious. "See, that's why I don't wanna tell you shit. Fuck you nigga." he stood up mad.

"My bad bro. So where she at?"

"Bitch left me to go back to the A." he answered shaking his head.

"Well, if you feeling her then I suggest you get yo bitch back."

"Oh, I am. I'mma go to the bitch school and if I gotta bust a cap in her teacher, dean, staff, whoever, then that's what I'mma do. But the bitch coming back with me." The nigga stood up and picked up his strap from the table. I fell out laughing because I could tell he was serious. He tucked his strap in his waistband and right then Candy walked back into the room.

"Layla Alliiii," Marco boasted egging on the situation.

"It was time bro."

"Wish I was here." He laughed. "I'm bout to catch a flight early in the morning so wait until I come back for round two." Marco spoke then headed for the door.

"Where you going?"

"Get my bitch back." he smirked then walked out. All I could do was shake my head.

"Come here ma." I looked at Candy and sighed. She walked over to me and I pulled her down onto my lap.

"I'm not fucking with you right now."

"Girl, you always fucking with me. Stop tripping. I know you mad, but right now, ma, it's too much going on. Don't let my dumb ass baby mama side track you from what's important. You seen the shit on the news CeCe." I called her the nickname Marco had given her.

"Did you fuck her?" she asked bypassing everything I had just said.

"You just missed everything I said yo."

"Just answer the fucking question my nigga." she was getting heated. I looked her in the eyes and I was about to tell her a bold-face lie.

"No ma. I haven't fucked her since I been fucking with you."

Sigh.

"So WHEN ARE you coming back son?" My granny asked concerned. She knew a nigga was a hot head and when I wanted something it was gonna be mines. After an hour of arguing with my G Moms I finally got her to understand that everything she said wasn't gonna work.

"I'll be back soon as I get her ma."

"Yeah, well what if she don't wanna come Marcell?"

"Ma, she ain't got a choice. Didn't we just talk about this?"

"Okay, okay," she sighed out clearly defeated. "You just be careful. And when you done make sure you bring her by so I could meet her. Because whoever she is she a special one."

"She is, granny, and I promise, soon as I'm done here, I'mma bring her to see you."

"Okay, you be safe. Love you."

"Love you, too, old lady." I told her and she discounted the line. I could understand how my granny felt because she knew me all too well. She knew a nigga was a firecracker so I couldn't blame her for being concerned. If anybody in the world knew me, my gmoms did. Shit, she's the one that raised me.

Pulling up to Morgan's school I hoped like hell I didn't miss her leaving. I had all the information I needed about her class schedule so I knew exactly what time her class let out. I was fifteen minutes late but I was gonna sit here until I spotted her. Morgan had a nigga fucked up. A nigga like me ain't never loved no bitch and here I was a thousand miles away, at a college campus with my strap on my passenger seat ready to set shit off. As I looked up, I noticed her walking out of a building that had the letter B on top. Right when I was gonna get out my whip some nigga ran up to catch her. He was clutching his backpack and he used his vacant hand to brush her hair back. Looking at the nigga he didn't seem like Morgan's type but with bitches you never know. Nigga looked like a straight bitch with his pants slightly rolled up at the bottom and his polo collar shirt.

He was wearing a chain but nothing major and his hair was in a low cut fade. The two began walking and Morgan hadn't even noticed me sitting here. Just the thought of this nigga fucking my bitch had me ready to body the both they ass right here.

I watched as he walked her to a 3 series 330i BMW. *Damn, my little baby rolling.* I thought watching them closely. He opened the door for her, then kissed her cheek before she climbed in. I was really hot. I shook my head continuously as I watched Morgan start her car and pull out the parking lot. As bad as I wanted to follow her, I didn't. I had something else in store for her snake ass.

⸻

The next morning, I checked out my hotel room and headed back to Morgan's school. The entire way there I was in deep thought. Just like last night, I tossed and turned all night; I couldn't get Morgan off my mind. I had plans for her; I just needed her to understand I was here and not going nowhere. That whole Plan B shit had fucked with my mental but I'm over it now. This go round I'mma put a baby in her and fuck what she talking about. But first, I had to convince her I was the nigga she needed in her life. Shit, I was the nigga any bitch needed.

I sat behind the tints of the whip I had rented. I made sure to park away because the factory tent wasn't as dark as I needed. I watched as Morgan pulled up and parked her whip. She exited the car then walked over to the many flowers that were aligned on the tree. She looked puzzled as she stopped to talk to two chicks that stood next to the tree. After moments went by, Morgan broke down falling to the ground. The girls she was talking to grabbed her off the ground and began rubbing her back to console her. Just watching her had me boiling inside. The pain in her face only confirmed what I already knew; she was fucking that nigga from yesterday.

Not being able to watch her break down over this nigga any longer, I hopped out the whip and walked towards where she stood. It's like everyone watched me as if they knew I didn't belong here, but I didn't give a fuck. When I walked up on her, she didn't turn right around but the look the girls were giving me caused her to look back. Her eyes grew wide but they looked broken. Tears streamed down her face as she looked at me.

"Mar... Marcell? What are you doing here?"

"Let's go Morgan."

"Whaaa...what you mean let's go?"

"Like I said ma, let's go."

"Marco, I can't just leave..." As she went to speak, I silenced her by showing my burner on my waistline. I wasn't gonna harm Morgan; I just wanted her to know I was serious. I was on her college campus with a strap. I knew Morgan like a book and she loved a nigga which meant she wasn't gonna want me to get caught up.

"Just go, Morg... I'll tell Mr. Smith you left because of..." the chick said then nodded her head towards the flowers. Morgan looked from the chick to me then back to the chick. The chick smiled to assure Morgan she was good but little did she know, I was snatching her ass up rather she liked it or not.

I walked off towards the rental and all I knew is, Morgan's ass better had been right behind me. When I climbed in, the passenger door opened and she slid into the seat not saying a word. I wished like hell the drive wasn't too long because I would have hopped on the highway. Instead I headed to the airport praying like hell I wouldn't have to hijack the plane to make this stubborn ass girl come with me.

"So what got you all shook up Morgan?" She looked out the window before answering.

"My friend was killed last night. It's crazy because he was so innocent; he didn't deserve to die."

"Did you fuck him?" I looked from the steering wheel to her.

"What do you mean did I fuck him?"

"Man, jus what I asked ma. Did you fuck the nigga?"

"No Marcell. We were just friends. We grew up together." I shot her a cold look.

"Well, not grew up together like that but we've been friends since ten." she spoke then began crying.

"So you really about to sit here and cry over another nigga in my car?"

"He was my fucking friend! And you got some nerves after you disowned me because I didn't want to have a fucking baby."

"You damn right. And one hunnit Morg, you're gonna have my seed sooner or later. Don't make be like them crazy white men in them movies and lock yo ass in a basement until you give birth."

"Your crazy boy."

"Watch yo fucking mouth. Ain't shit *boy* about me and soon I'mma have to show your ass." I told her then looked back towards the road. Morgan thought this shit was a game. I swear, I didn't want to start acting like them crazy psycho niggas in movies and I was hoping she didn't take me there.

"Why are we here?" she asked looking out the window.

"We going home ma."

"Fuck you mean?" she asked trying to get sassy.

I laughed it off because that shit was an act. After fucking with Morgan for some time I figured her out. This fast girl, street chick shit wasn't her. Morgan was square as an L7. Baby girl got a thrill out of hood niggas but that's exactly what it was, a thrill. If she was so street like she proclaimed, then a street nigga would have been bust her little pussy open. Wasn't no virgins in the hood dawg and her, yeah baby was indeed a virgin before she let me hit it.

"Ma, please don't make this shit hard. I need you to come with me. We'll be back for your things."

"Wait, wait, wait. So are you like kidnapping me or something?" her face frowned up.

"If that's what you wanna call it. But you're getting on this plane one way or another." I shot her a look that told her I wasn't playing so she opened her door and got out pouting.

As I SAT on the plane I couldn't help but look over at Marcell. His handsome face held so much pain and I'm more than sure it came from my rejection. No lie the way he came for me was sexy as hell but this wasn't the way to get me back. I knew because of what happened to Phillip I could get an excuse on grievance but that would only last a week. I was gonna take my ass back home and deal with my parents because I knew after today if Marcell didn't kill me, my parents sure in the hell would.

He has a little game that he plays
Clever little ways and a hot boy style
Brags about the dough that he makes
Flash a little cash most girls wild out

Mya 'Best of Me' played in my headphone as I looked out the window. The sun was going down so the sky looked orange and purple. Looking into the clouds, I thought of Phil. Tears began to pour from my eyes; I was an emotional wreck. Phil and I had known each other for years and we were extremely close. I didn't have many friends at school except Lola and Carmen and other than them two it was always Phil and I. We did everything together. He was so cool and innocent. Whoever murdered him I prayed like hell they would rot in hell. Phil and I had never did anything together, however we did teach each other how to kiss.

I laughed to myself at the thought and Marcell shot me an evil glare. This nigga was starting to creep me out. I swear it was something in his eyes that told me he was guilty of something but I let it ride. I had enough on my plate at the moment. Lola had mentioned to me that Phil was found dead in his dorm with three bullets to the chest and one to the head. What puzzled me was Phil didn't bother nobody nor was he in any gangs or anything. I was gonna miss my friend and his big, beautiful smile dearly.

Getting off the plane, Marcell and I headed to his car that was parked in the overnight parking. He still hasn't said much to me and I was fine with that because I was still trying to process everything. My best friend was dead and my so-called boyfriend had basically kidnapped me. Marcell's phone rang and he looked at me before picking up.

"Yes, I got her." he said to the caller. I couldn't hear what they were saying but what I did know was the shit sounded weird. Thoughts of him killing me ran through my head but I didn't do anything to deserve that so just as fast as I thought it, it left my mind.

"Who was that?" I asked as I climbed into his car.

"Don't matter." he spoke then turned up his music. Like always, he played Lil Durks *India* but right now the song didn't mean shit to me. This nigga had me all the way over here for what? To treat me like shit. I don't think he realized I was going through a lot right now. Instead of him comforting me, he was dismissing me like some random hoe.

I sat back in the chair and tuned Marcell out. The drive was a nice lengthy one so I busied myself on social media. I had to leave Facebook because it was to sad. Every other pic was of Phil with *RIP* on the side of his name and that shit was stressing me more. I went back to Instagram and just looked through the explore pics. Moments later, Marcell and I pulled up to a very huge home. The house looked older and the neighborhood didn't look too upscale. I mean it wasn't the hood but it was home either.

When he got out the car, he came around and opened my door. I looked from him to the home and I was a bit nervous.

"Man bring yo stupid ass on." he said then walked towards the home. I slowly climbed out and closed the door behind me. When I got to the door, the smell of oxtails and cabbage was seeping through and my stomach growled. Finally realizing I haven't ate today, I hoped like hell whoever was cooking would at least give Marcell a plate so I can eat off of it.

When we walked in, the house was dimly lit and quiet. The only sound heard was the sound of pots and pans being shuffled around. The outside of the home didn't do the house any justice because the inside was gorgeous. It was huge and nicely decorated. The china cabinet alone looked expensive and even the chaise chairs in the hall looked nice and modern. Marcell grabbed my hand and guided me to the back. We entered the kitchen and there was an older lady standing over the stove. She looked up and the smile plastered on her face was priceless.

"Morgan, baby." she smiled and walked over to give me a hug.

"Damn, grandma, that's all you see?"

"Oh boy hush." she laughed playfully hitting him with hand mitt.

"I'm bout to go shower." He kissed his grandmother on the cheek then came over to me.

"Granny gone feed you; I be back aight?" I nodded my head yes. *Finally he was being nice.* I thought then walked over to take a seat.

"Girl that grandson of mines is something else." she shook her head. "I'mma tell you this and don't say I told you but that boy is in love with you chile. Marcell has never brought a woman here and after the shit he pulled today, I know that nigga loves you." she said sounding slang. I couldn't do shit but laugh.

"Yes, he's something else, Ms. Foster." I said calling her by her married name. A few times Marcell had spoken on his grandmother so it was like I had already knew her.

"Oh dear call me G moms or Granma."

"Okay." I giggle.

"You want some food?"

"Yes. I'm starving." I rubbed my stomach. She began moving around the kitchen preparing three plates that I assumed was for the two of us and Marcell.

"Morgan, when a man loves you he won't give up. He'll do anything in his power to have you and he won't let anybody stand in his way." She looked at me with a look that I couldn't read. It was like she was speaking to me with her eyes and that shit too was weird.

"I love him grandma; it's just...it's complicated." I sighed. "I just wanna finish school you know? I owe it to my parents." I grabbed my plate out of her hand. Right there at the countertop I began to eat because I didn't want to go to the dinner table alone.

"My grandson could be very demanding at times but he means no harm. He's very kind-hearted but I'mma tell you this, that boy loves you so love him with every ounce of you because you don't want to regret it in the end. Like I said, he's never been in love and for the shit he did with you, he's loving hard Morgan." she said then walked over to grab Marcell's plate. She walked it to the back then came back in minutes.

"He wants you. Fourth door to the left." she said and grabbed my plate that I was done with. I washed my hands then headed down the long hall. When I got to the door, I pushed it open and Marcell was sitting on the bed eating his food. He was now wearing some b-ball shorts, no shirt and a pair of socks. On the side of him was a big t-shirt, a extra pair of socks, a bar of Dove soap and towels that I assumed was for me. I picked up the items and headed for the shower that was attached to the room.

———

I tried my hardest not to cry in this shower. My emotions were all over the place. I thought of Phil constantly but Marcell was interfering with those thoughts. The words that his granny spoke played over and over in my mind and they were bitter sweet. *That boy loves you so love him with every ounce of you because you don't want to regret it.* The part of Marcell loving made me feel great inside but right now I was confused. At this point, I didn't know where we would go from here. *How would he react when I go back home?* I thought but my thoughts came to an end.

The glass door slid open and Marcell stood there naked as the day he was born. His body was rippled and he had his locks pinned up to the top of his head. Without invitation .he stepped in and pulled me into his arms. For the first time since I've been in his presence, I felt at ease. I laid my head on his chest and I couldn't help it. Tears began to pour from my eyes. I wept, I sobbed as the tears flowed down his chest blending into the currents of the water. Marcell lifted my chin and demanded I looked him in the eyes. Seductively, he kissed my lips. Now this was a side of Marcell I had never seen. He was gentle with me. The rough interior was slowly becoming submissive. It was like he craved me intensively.

After the intense kiss, he began tracing kisses down my chest to my already hardened nipples. Taking one into his mouth, he sucked it as I held onto his locks for dear life. In one swift move, he picked me up and positioned me on the shower wall. The way my body jumped I guess he could tell the wall was cold so he turned the shower towards us and let the hot water wet us entirely. He then looked me in the eyes and again he pecked my lips. Looking at Marcell right now was like a dream come true. All those days without him it felt like I was dying inside. I constantly thought of him but was too scared to call.

"I love you, Morgan Blake Leigh." he said calling me by my entire name. I was so caught up in the moment I didn't respond. Tears came pouring down my face again, however this time I pulled him close to me. I grabbed his large penis and held it in my hand. Thoughts of the last time we made love played in my mind. I knew I couldn't ask for a plan b this time so it was for the gusto. I positioned him at my entrance and began winding my hips slowly. I could feel the precum building up on his tip. Not being able to help myself, I pushed him further inside of me. I winced as it went in because Marcell was extremely big in size.

"Damn, ma, you miss a nigga huh?" he asked with a look on his face like he was in heaven.

"Yes, I miss you. Ahhhh. I miss you so muchhh." I moaned out as our body began to form a rhythm that we moved in.

"You gone stay with daddy forever?" he asked without missing a beat. As he went in and out of me, he began to suck my tits hungrily.

"Yessss." I cried out. I could feel the penetration of his shaft going in and out of me wetting my tunnel more and more. Although we were in the water, the feeling of my wetness was different. In so little time, he had me exploding. My warm juices ran down his legs but he never stopped.

"Promise you'll never leave." he whispered into my ear as he began to stroke harder.

"I promise." I kissed him passionately. "Ohh, shit, bae I promise. Please don't stop, ohhhh shit please don't stop." I begged for more. He began pulverizing my insides and because I was pinned on the wall I did my best to keep up. I didn't know what I was doing but I mean how hard was it to match his thrust.

"You gone give me a baby Morgan because daddy not pulling out ma? Shiiiit, I'm not pulling out." he pounded harder and harder. I began squeezing my muscles and I could feel my pussy clamping down on his dick. The heart beat in the tip of his head told me he was about to cum. He began grunting loudly; I knew his granny had to hear us. Twirling my hips I let him have his way with me.

"Cum in this pussy daddy. I'mma give you a baby." I seductively whispered in his ear. I prayed like hell it wasn't the dick talking for me but something told me this was where I would be forever. At this moment, it didn't matter what my parents had to say, how Cambree felt; hell I didn't even care if Grandma walked in. I was in love and I wanted this feeling to last forever.

"I'll be back Margret." I shouted towards the back room where the nanny was occupied with Blessing. I quickly grabbed my car keys and hurried out the door. When I hopped in, I put on my Mary J CD and backed out the spiral driveway as fast as I could. I needed to be gone before Major came home. I knew what I was about to do was thirsty but I didn't care. I'd been doing it every day since the day I saw her in the mall. I went from being a happily married woman to an obsessed, torn, stalker. And as bad as I wanted to confront Major, I just couldn't bring myself to doing it. Sooner or later, I would have that woman to woman talk and once she confessed then I would have to bring it to Major's attention.

I knew I'd be gambling with my life but I was more than sure she would reveal herself. The only thing holding me back was Camiere. I still didn't know how she felt about what went down with us so I had to stay clear of her for now.

She said it's your child
And it really messed me up

How could you deny
Your own flesh and blood

As Mary J sung the lyrics to 'Your Child' my heart broke with every lyric. Thoughts of the little girl played over in my mind and that shit hurt my heart to the core. Pulling up to the home that Camiere once shared with his mother, so many memories flashed through my mind of the day Ms. Leigh had the 4th of July picnic and Cambree showed up with Major as her date. I knew after that night, nothing would ever be the same. And to add injury to insult, Kaliyah showed up and made things between Camiere and I worse than they already were.

Sitting outside the home, I watched from across the street as Cambree repeatedly dialed a number on her cell. Her facial expression showed concern but whatever it was, she was worried. The gangsta in me wanted to pull out my 40 Glock and start shooting but the mother in me decided to spare her.

Ring!

My phone nearly scared me to death. Looking at the caller ID I almost didn't answer.

"Hello?"

"So are we set for tomorrow?" Candy asked referring to the BBQ we were having tomorrow.

"Umm, yeah... I guess."

"Yanese! What is yo ass doing?" she screamed into the phone.

"Nothing..."

"You're *nothing* ass is lying. I know you not over there again?" she asked already knowing. It's like I was infatuated with stalking this bitch and Candy knew. I spent most of my days searching her life online. I had found out everything about her from where she lived to her new tattoo shop located on South Beach.

"Nah, I'm at the store getting the rest of the stuff." I lied.

Constantly, Candy tried to talk me out of the thoughts of the baby being Major's, but I wasn't buying it. It was like I could feel it in my gut this baby was his. Most women would call me crazy but you wouldn't understand if you haven't been down this road.

"Okay, well I'll meet you at your house. I need some girl therapy." she sighed.

"Okay, ma. I'll be there in about twenty minutes."

"Okay." she said, and I disconnected the line. I started the ignition to my car and made an illegal U-Turn towards my home. I knew I would be back but for now I would give this shit a break. It was like I was stressing myself out more.

⸺

It was the day of the BBQ and I had a pounding ass headache from staying up all night taking shots with Candy. We both had issues in our life fucking with these BME niggas. Though our situations were different, we both had baby mama issues that were driving us crazy. It was already too much going on with the empire, so we didn't need the extra stress. Major and I had taken a big loss with the drugs that were confiscated and not to mention the shit with the police and Cap. The way BME was moving I could tell shit was about to get wild. They tried their hardest to keep me out the loop of the pig war but no matter how hard they tried my nosey ass always found out.

Walking outside with the pan of chicken that was ready to go on the grill, I ran into Marco.

"My bad sis. Let me help you with that." he said and grabbed the pan out my hand.

"Thank you Marco." I smiled and looked over to the girl he had on his shoulder. She was really cute and the way she slightly hid behind him I could tell she was shy.

"Hi, I'm Yanese, and you are?" I extended my hand. She looked me in the face and it was something about her look that confused me.

"I'm... I'm... Morgan." she tried to smile but she also wore a shocked expression causing both Marco and I to look at one another. For a minute I thought I was tripping but because he caught the look I knew I wasn't.

"Do I know you?"

"Um...no, no....you're just really pretty." she finally smiled.

"Aww, thanks...you're really pretty too."

"Thank you." she blushed. "Do you need help with anything?" she asked.

"I like her already Marco." I nubbed his arm. "Everything is pretty much done. Let's grab a drink and go chill under the tent." I told her and pulled her away from Marco. Marco walked over to the grill and handed the pan of chicken to the cook. He then walked over to where Major and Brent were.

"So are you guys serious?" I asked Morgan the moment we took a seat under the tent.

"I mean I really like him."

"Like?" I asked smirking.

"Okay, not like." she giggled. "I love that man. It's just complicated because he's..he's.."

"Hard to handle?" I finished her sentence.

"Yessss."

"Yeah I agree but he's a really good little nigga."

"Yanni!!!" I looked over to Dajah who was screaming my name. I stood up to give her a hug.

"I miss you!" I cooed as I pinched her shoulder.

"Hey Jigga."

"Sup sis." We hugged and he headed over to the fellas.

"Dajah, this is Morgan, Marcos' girlfriend, Morgan, this is Marcos' cousin, Dajah."

"Nice to meet you Morgan. How the hell you end up with his ass?" Dajah asked and we all laughed.

"Man y'all bet not be over here talking bout a nigga." Marco walked up out of nowhere. "And y'all really bet not be corrupting my bitch head over here." his ass said and took a seat.

Morgan dismissed the fact he called her a bitch. Instead, she blushed and accepted his invite of him cuddling up underneath her. When I felt some hands approach my shoulder and began massaging me I didn't have to look up. The smell of Major's Creed cologne filled my nose making me melt just like Morgan. Lately, I've been mad at his ass but the way he fucked me last night until the early morning had a bitch head gone. I lifted my head to meet with his lips and placed a juicy kiss on them.

"Y'all gay." Marco said laughing.

"Shut yo in love ass up." I threw the napkin at him I had balled up in my hand.

"Where the fuck this nigga Trig at?" Major asked but more so talking to himself.

"Shit, last I knew he was going to pick up some shit for the function." Marco replied speaking of the BME party that was gonna go up next month. This party was gonna be big and I couldn't wait. The team was so bossed up this party was announced all over the radio and everybody from all over the world attended. BME had really taken over and was well-respected. Who would have ever thought that little ol me would build an empire that took over the world and became the most talked about. Just because I slightly fell back from the game and passed it to Major, I still held the crown and took the credit.

I pulled out my phone to place a call to Candy. This wasn't like her ass to not be on time. She was very punctual and wouldn't miss this picnic for the world. As I began to dial, my phone rang displaying her number. I answered and I could barely hear anything she was saying.

"On, gaaa. On God.." she was screaming. "I'mma kill this bitch!"

"Wait, I can barely understand you. What's wrong?" I jumped to my feet and screamed into the phone. I could feel everyone's eyes on me trying to find out the same thing.

"The nail shop! Oh my God." she began to sob. "The nail shop is gone....." she cried harder.

"Bae, what's up?" Major asked. I didn't know what Candy meant but whatever it was, was serious. I passed the phone to Major in hopes he could calm her down. It didn't take no time for him to find out what was gonna.

"We on our way." he said then hung the phone up. When I looked over, Marco had his gun out and I couldn't do shit but smile. This damn boy was too much.

"What's up big bro?" he asked Major.

"Somebody burnt the nail shop down." Major replied then looked to me. I cocked my head to the side like *are you fucking serious*. I then quickly ran into the house to tell the nanny we be back and grabbed my bag.

"I wanna go with you Nee Nee." Majesty ran up to me. I kissed his little forehead and bent down to tell him.

"I gotta go see about aunty Candy baby. I need you to be a big boy and help nanny with your brother and sister baby. Okay? Can you do that for me?" he shook his head yes without responding. I nudged the top of his head and smiled. I loved this kid as if he was my own. His hoe ass mom basically sold him to us and because I loved Major I chose to take on the role of his parent. I really didn't mind because Majesty loved me like his own.

I walked back outside and looked around to my crew. Everyone waited for me to move and this shit made me wanna get back in the field. I gave the streets up to be a wife and raise my kids but it seems like over these last few months so much was forcing my hand. I just prayed I could keep copacetic.

I grasped the game in so little time, and thanks to Black, I learned to adapt with ease. Don't let me give all praises to Black because

Sebastian had left me with a heavy heart. He's the main reason I was the way I was now. I don't wanna get all into details about him because he's really a sore spot for me. Just know, if he was here, I'd kill his ass myself.

19 / CANDY

IN A STATE OF SHOCK, I stood here and watched my business go up in flames. The top was now burning and the bottom was already burnt to a crisp. I tried so hard to contain my anger but I couldn't help it. I was stomping, mad and punching walls. I'm talking to the point my knuckles were bleeding. I wanted so bad to kill some shit right now, and I'm talking anybody could get it.

We had been here twenty-five minutes and the fire was untamable. Like a baby, I cried, I fought and gave up. My shit was gone, and I couldn't cry over spilled milk. However, I could kill me a muthafucka, then I would feel better.

For some reason, Trig's bitch ass baby mama was the one to blame. I wasn't stupid by far. Jasmyne's bitch ass was behind this and I was about to go to her house and go haywire. I knew I couldn't kill the bitch based on her having Trig's daughter but I was about to hurt the bitch something serious.

"Oh, my God, Candy!" I stopped pacing and looked over at Yanese as she ran towards me shouting.

"It was that bitch Yanese." I told her still pacing. "I know it was her. I don't have enemies, I don't make enemies." I started crying right when Marco and Boss ran over to me.

"Sis, what the fuck happened yo?" Marco asked looking from me to the top of the building where the flames seemed to be growing. His facial expression was worse than Boss' and, like always, he scared me.

"I don't know...no, fuck that I do know!...it was that bitch Jasmyn. I know it was her Marco." I stormed away then right back to him. I was really pacing and hot as a pressing comb on the stove for 60 seconds.

Fuck this shit, I thought storming towards my car.

Without saying a word to anyone, I pulled off in a rage. In a normal forty-minute minute drive, I was to my destination in less than twenty. I hopped out my car and ran to the front door of the home my man bought and paid all the bills at. I knocked so hard I shook the stone-made home forcefully. Moments later, I was hit with the surprise of my life. Trig answered the door wearing only his draws. He wore a scowl on his face because I'm sure he wondered who was knocking so hard. Now that we were face to face, the nigga's eyes grew wide and he wore a look as if he knew he was caught. I wasn't tripping off the fact that this nigga was here but why the fuck was he in his briefs? I pulled out my little friend that was intended for Jasmyn and went haywire. I stuck Trig right in his fucking arm missing his neck.

"Forreal, you gone stab a nigga?" he asked more shocked than in pain.

"You damn right, nigga, fuck you!" I tried to attack him again but he shoved me to the ground. Moments later, Jasmyn walked in and the moment I saw the bitch I jumped to my feet and ran up on her. The bitch didn't stand a chance. I swung my steak knife furiously stabbing her repeatedly. Blood began to quirt and the bitch was screaming for dear life.

"That's enough, Candy!" Trig tackled me to the ground. I tried my hardest to fight his ass but I couldn't. My emotions began to take over me and I began sobbing.

"That...that bii...that bitch burned down my fucking nail shop and you protecting this hoe." I looked over at Jasmyn who laid on the floor covered in blood. She looked as if she was going in and out of conscious and I didn't give two fucks.

"Trig, baby, I ....please, I need an ambulance." she said barely being able to speak. She was holding her arm but the bitch should have been holding her shoulder because that shit was leaking.

"Man, go Candy." he shook his head and stood to his feet.

"Fuck you and that bitch. Make sure you come get yo shit too. And since this where you wanna be, have my muthafucking money for a new muthafucking shop. FUCK INSURANCE!" I spit the biggest loogie in his face that he dodged and it landed on his shoulder. I stormed out the house feeling much better but the fact still remained, my man was caught cheating and bigger than that, my fucking business was burnt to crisp. I couldn't do shit but bang my hands on my steering wheel and cry my eyes out. Trig and I had been through so much in so little time, I thought I was his rock. I guess the saying is true, 'niggas will always fuck they baby mama'.

I mean, damn, I was his Trap Gyrl. I've been the bitch by his side when shit got rocky. I cooked, cleaned, sucked his dick good, cooked his dope and even gave him some ass. I don't even like ass jobs because that shit hurt. I gave this nigga all of me. And for what? To only get my heart broke.

―――

Trig

A nigga felt fucked up right now. My BM was stabbed the fuck up but all I could think about was Candy catching a nigga over her crib like she did. How the fuck was I gonna explain being in my draws? A gullible bitch would have went for that shit, but nah, not Candy. Just the thought of her face when I opened the door hurt me. I couldn't believe she stabbed me, but I deserved it. And to keep it one hunnit, Jas deserved that shit, too.

Right after the ambulance picked Jas up, Marco called me and told me the shop was indeed burnt down. When it all registered, Jas had left me at her crib talking bout she be right back. Because I never question her whereabouts, I didn't even ask where she was going. It was something about the way she dressed but something like this would not have dawned on me. When she got back, she was acting weird as fuck, too, so Marco confirmed the allegations Candy made against Jas. I already had a lot going on and this shit was about to get deeper.

"Do you hear me?!" Jas shouted bringing me from a daze. I looked over at her annoyed because this shit was all her fault. "You keep defending this bitch. What about me?"

"What about you Candy? I mean, Jas." I shook my head. I was bugging.

"Wow. Forreal Trayon?" she started crying more than she was.

"My bad for calling you that, but Jas, this shit yo fault. You did that dumb shit and it was unnecessary. You know how much money you cost me?"

"Oh, so you gone pay for it?"

"You damn right. That's my bitch, my nigga."

"Was yo bitch."

"I mean, let's be for real. Did you think this little stunt was gonna make me be back with you?"

"No ,but that bitch shouldn't have put her fucking hands on me. And in front of my fucking baby."

"Man, I'm out. You a dizzy ass bitch I swear yo. Call me when you discharging so I can pay your bill. Other than that, don't bother me." I said then walked out the door. This bitch was looney as fuck. She complaining about Candy putting hands on her but she deserved it because she came to our crib calling her out her name.

From the other side, I could hear Jas screaming for me to come back but that shit went over my head. I was officially done with her. And since Candy was done with me, a nigga was single shit. Maybe that's how shit needed to be. I've been dealing with this shit so long a nigga was tired. Being by myself was prolly best. Especially right now when shit was getting hectic in these streets.

When I pulled up to the crib I shared with Candy, I walked in and went straight for our bedroom. I was gonna pack a bag so I could go stay at a hotel. It was no point in arguing with her because she made herself clear. Upon entering the room, I felt worse than before. She was sitting on the bed, silently crying as her body rocked back and forth. For the first time, I regret being with her. I loved her to death but because a nigga couldn't do right, it was making me regret hurting her.

Candy looked up and we locked eyes. I could see the hurt in them and the look she gave me was much different from earlier. This time she looked broken. She looked stressed. And I could see the exhaustion all over her face. *She tired of my shit,* I thought quickly turning my head to proceed towards the closet. To my surprise, my things were still hung up neatly. I began pulling clothes off hangers as quickly as I could. I needed to get away from her and fast. Being in Candy's presence was making me weak.

I turned the lock to my safe and before I could enter the last number, there was a loud crash. Candy and I both looked at each other. We both quickly ran to the front room and...

"FREEZE!!!"

I looked at Candy and I knew I was going to jail. It was only a matter of time before the Cartel rolled over on my ass. Once again, I had failed my baby. I threw my hands up in surrender because I didn't want to be another dead nigga.

"Candice Candy Paul! You're under arrest." one officer spoke walking over to her slapping the cuffs on her. She didn't bother to say one word. She surrendered herself with ease. She looked at me with a blank stare and held my gaze for a few moments.

"I'm coming to get you." I told her meaning every word I said.

"Don't bother. I got it." she said and rolled her eyes. Candy walked out the door before the officers were even ready to escort her out. The way she sashayed out confirmed what I already knew again; this bitch was seriously not fucking with me.

———

"How'd you..."

"Surprise, surprise little bitch."

"Look, if you thugs are here to rob me just take my money and go. Please don't hurt me or my family."

"Oh, we're for sure gonna kill you but not until we ask you a few questions."

"I'm a cop. If you kill me... someone... someone will find out." this nigga began stuttering.

"I know this nigga did not..." Marco said looking at the pig.

"Awe, shit." I yelled out disgusted and put my shirt over my nose as if it would protect the smell.

"Nasty ass nigga shitted on himself." Marco got a kick out the shit.

"Brahhhh, let's hurry up. I can't take this smell too long."

"Plee...plee..please don't kill me."

"Just tell us what happened to our boy Cap?"

"Cap? I don't know a Cap." Before I could say anything, Marco fired a shot into his knee cap.

"Grrrrrr," the nigga growled so loud it echoed through the room.

"Nigga, you the one that arrested him. So yo bitch ass know exactly who he is." I raised my gun to fire another shot.

"Wait, wait, wait...I'll tell you. Please don't kill me."

"You got five seconds bitch."

"It was King Cam." the nigga blurted out. Because Cam was in jail and Cap was arrested, it all made perfect sense. And it also meant that Cap was set up. This bitch right in front of us arrested Cap to set him up.

"You bitch!" I eyed the pig with hatred then sent five shots into his chest. As bad as I wanted to torture him this nigga had to go.

"I wanted to kill his ass." Marco whined like a crazed psychopath.

"Man, bring yo ass on nigga." I punched him in the arm and headed out the door.

Once we were in the whip, we sped off towards the dump. The dump is where we dumped cars, guns and anything else we needed to get rid of. We made one call and it was disposed of.

"Man, what's up with sis?" Marco asked referring to Candy. I really didn't know how to answer so I kept it gutta.

"Shit, she ain't fucking with me."

"Man, she a savage yo. I knew it was only a matter of time before she gave Jas dumb ass the business."

"Shit stupid as fuck though. Now Jas pressing charges and shit."

"Let me just kill her." Marco looked at me with a serious expression.

"Nigga, that's my baby mama."

"And she on some snitch shit. The bitch burnt sis shit down and now she wanna play victim."

"Man, I'mma handle the shit."

"You just make sure that bitch don't go to court." he said then got quiet. For a few moments, we drove silently. To break the ice, I was the first one to speak.

"We gotta get that bitch next. Brent bitch ass sleeping on the job. Every time I ask him about the hoe he start stuttering and shit. I think that nigga falling in love with her."

"Just let me kill the nigga."

"Yo ass always wanna kill somebody."

"That nigga snaking us. I can feel it bro."

"Boss keep saying the same shit. I'mma look into it and see what's up with him."

"You ready for the party?" I asked getting off subject. I didn't want to discuss Brent any further because a part of me could tell the change in him. This nigga knew too much of our operation so if I found out he was on some fuck shit I was gonna kill him myself.

"Hell, yeah, got me some beaver fur. A nigga gone be fresh to death." We both chuckled.

"This nigga and his fur." I shook my head.

"Nigga, you rock fur, too."

"Yeah, but yo ass rock them even in the summer."

"Cause I'm that nigga." he spoke cockily. We laughed and went over the details for the party. This shit was gonna be big and I couldn't wait.

"WHAT ARE YOU DOING HERE? You can't be here."

"Fuck you mean I can't be here." I asked unsure of what she meant. She kept looking back as if she was gonna get caught up or some shit.

"Brent, baby, you can't be here."

"Why Vee? You said you was leaving that nigga?" I asked now frustrated. I pushed past her and invited myself in. Even if the nigga was here, I would pop his ass and get on. I wasn't playing with Veronica. Bitch had a nigga open and now she had been playing with a nigga. It's been four days since I've talked to her and she wasn't answering none of my calls. Which was the reason I was here today.

Ever since the night I smashed, Veronica and I had been kicking it tough. We've been out quite a few times, I've fucked every chance we got, and her pretty ass even had me on the phone all night talking bout all that girly shit. Let's not fail to mention I wasn't giving none of my bitches the time of day. Hell, I was even dodging Mercedes.

"Look, I have something to tell you." She wore a worried expression.

"Man, I don't even wanna hear it really. I told her sensing it had to do with her occupation. Veronica didn't know I knew her identity and to be honest that shit didn't bother me anymore. I knew I was wrong because the purpose of hooking up with her was to kill her but a nigga couldn't help but fall for her ass. I knew Boss was gonna be pissed but that shit didn't matter because soon I was gonna be King. You heard right. I was gonna sit on the throne and run BME my damn self. My plan was to eventually kill Boss Major and take his bitch. I loved the fuck out of Yanese so she would be the Queen that rode out into the sunset with a nigga.

"You have to hear this. Have a seat." I looked behind me and when I saw a stool I took a seat. I pulled her arm. She tried to resist but when I had her on my lap I started planting kisses on her neck. She liked that shit.

"Ohh, baby, not right now. Please we need..." she was cut off by a sexy moan. "Oooh..."

"You like that shit huh?"

"Yes..but I..I can't do..." I shhhh'd her by kissing her. I tore her top off and picked her up into my arms. I walked around the house until I found her bedroom. I used my foot to kick open the door then headed for the bed. I aggressively kissed her as I tore the rest of her clothing off.

"You don't miss a nigga, Vee?"

"Yes, baby. Yes, I miss you."

"So why I haven't heard from you in a few days? You don't miss this dick?" As I spoke into her ear, I entered her with two fingers. Going in and out, all you could hear is smacking throughout the room. Her shit was wet and her juices was pouring out like a faucet. "This pussy wet as fuck ma."

"It's wet for you baby. Oooh, it's wet for you." she purred. I wanted so bad to fuck the shit out of her but fuck that, I needed to try and hook her ass. One thing I never did was eat her pussy. Hell, the only bitch pussy I ate was Cedes and that explained why the bitch was acting like she was.

"Lay back, baby." I told her as I pushed her upper body down to lay flat. I then spread her legs and bent down into her pussy. I sniffed that muthafucka long and hard. Her shit smells like pineapples or some shit. Satisfied, I took my first lick and made sure to savor the moment.

"Baby, stop teasing me." she whined.

"Tell me you love me."

"You know I love you." she said but that was a lie. We only been fucking a few months and after every session she would run off. Not to mention, she never even mentioned the word love.

"Tell me you love me, Veronica." I told her putting my entire mouth on her clit. I folded my tongue to fit her clit perfectly. I began gyrating my tongue and instantly her body began to shake.

"I love you..oh, my God, I love you!" she screamed out. That's all I needed to hear. It was now showtime.

⊏⊐

"So what was it you wanted to tell me?" I asked as I rubbed my hands through Veronica's hair. She laid on my chest and because of her silence I could tell she had something on her mind. She raised up and looked at me with so much concern.

"Look, Brent. I'mma gonna tell you this because I really like you." She looked at me so I nodded my head for her to continue.

"I'm not who you think I am. I..I..I work for NYPD." she blurted out then dropped her head. There was a short pause before she finally looked up.

"I already know, ma."

"You do?"

"Yes. I actually have something to tell you." I confessed.

"I'm listening."

"I'm not a pharmacy tech, ma. I lied. I'm actually part of a crew that you have been trying to take down"

"BME?" she whispered unsurely. I nodded my head yes. She jumped up and began rambling. I jumped up behind her and she backed away from me as if I would harm her.

"Man, chill. I'm not gonna hurt you, Vee. I know all this shit is crazy but trust me there's a good explanation for it."

"How the fuck...what the fuck...nigga, what explanation do you have as to why you didn't tell me. So if you knew, then you were sent to?" Oh, my God. She started crying. I ran to her side and pulled her into my arms. I know it was wrong but a nigga had developed some strong feeling for her so I had to console her. I knew I was going against the grain by telling her who I was, however I prayed she would help me out with my plan. In this game, everyone was a pawn and everyone was being used. The only two that ended up on top was the king and queen and as long as the queen protected the king, the king could reign.

Veronica

"You falling for that nigga?"

"No."

"You a fucking lie man."

"If I was so what. You don't want me."

"You muthafucking right I don't! Bitch, you ain't shit but a hoe. You was supposed to fuck this nigga to get in good not fall in love."

"So basically you used me?"

"Man, you know what it is. You not my type of bitch Veronica."

"Why, because you so caught up over that bitch!?" I nodded towards the bible that sat beside his bed. "Yeah, you think I don't know. You stare at her fucking picture all day every fucking day. What is it? I'm not pretty enough?"

"Man, gone with that shit!"

"You're a fucking sucka. That bitch put you away and, thanks to me, you're a free man."

"Bitch, you better watch your fucking mouth." He ran up on me and yoked me up. As he held me around my neck, tears poured from my eyes. I felt so foolish. I felt like everything I did was for nothing. This man didn't want me. He was still in love with Yanese, and I had to come to terms with it.

I pried his hands from around my neck then fixed my blouse. I was done trying to love this man. Yes, I was falling for Brent but that was out of the lack of love I received from Cam. All he did was abuse my pussy and talk to me as if I wasn't shit. I thought that after helping him become a free man, we would ride off into the sunset but this nigga had other plans. He constantly talked about revenge on Yanese, but that nigga wasn't fooling me. I could tell he was still in love by the way he stared at her photo. He thought I didn't know he had a picture of her hidden inside of a bible. The same bible he brought home from jail. Many days, I stood by his cell and watched him in a daze as he lusted over her picture. This nigga was obsessed with a bitch who left him to rot in hell.

"Don't ever mention that bitch again, or I'mma kill you right along with her." he snatched my shirt.

"You ain't gone kill that bitch!" I spat as I snatched away from him.

I gave him one last look and shook my head. I walked away from him and I didn't plan on coming back. As of today, this man was dead to me just like Boss was years ago. The worst thing in the world was to have to walk away from someone you loved dearly, and for the second time, I have been played by a nigga who was in love with the same bitch.

⸻

I walked into my office at work and before I could sit down, Sergeant Cooper had ordered me to his office. When I walked in, he was on the phone so I took a seat. Moments later, he hung up and began to speak.

"Ms. Nelson, have you seen or spoken to Andrew?"

"No sir."

"Well, I'm starting to get worried about him. This isn't like Andrew to miss any days. I'mma swing by his home and check things out." He stood to his feet and put on his hat.

"Okay, I have some paperwork to catch up on." I headed to my office now worrying about Andrew. Sarge was right; this wasn't like Andrew. I don't know why I had a gut feeling that BME had something to do with this and my gut also told me I should not have let Sarg go alone.

Sitting at my desk, I pulled out my iPhone and went to my camera app. I lustfully watched Cam as he dropped his clothing getting ready to take a shower. You damn right I had the apartment bugged and camera wired that I had moved Cam into. I was obsessed with this man. Any chance I got I'd play with my love box watching him sleep. Since he's been home, he only made love to me once. Between Yanese and BME, it was all Cam was worried about. Now that Cam had pretty much said fuck me, I was gonna get my revenge on Yanese's bitch ass then be with Brent. As far as Cam was concerned, I was gonna let him be. I was more than sure after I killed that bitch Yanese he would rot in hell with her.

"Hello?" I answered my ringing phone. Of course it was Brent. He called me every hour on the hour. Because of my mixed emotions, it was basically bitter sweet. I was bitter because of the heart break I had just sustained from Cam, but it was sweet how baby was right here to make me feel better. A part of me felt bad because I was only supposed to fuck Brent and lead him to my trap. Or should I say Cam's trap.

BME was moving reckless. I think they forgot I was a cop. I had everyone's operation bugged per Andrew and I. One day BME had slipped up on a phone convo about how they were gonna set me up. The plot was for Brent to follow me, fuck me and kill me. I faked my drunkness and even knew I was gonna fuck him. Since the day we were watching BME, I thought Brent was sexy as hell. And now I knew he had good dick to go with his sexiness. It was cute how Cam acted jealous. I mean, it was my pussy so it was my business. He wanted Brent dead but Brent and I had already formed a plan. Therefore, I was gonna ride this shit out.

"Sup, baby?"

"Hey." I spoke dryly. I wasn't upset or anything; a bitch just didn't have any energy after Cam.

"We on for tomorrow right?"

"Yes." I assured him.

"Wyd? You miss me?"

"What else. I do have a job Brent." We both laughed.

"Yeah, you right. But after a nigga make this move you won't have to work."

"Awe, baby," I smiled into the phone.

"Ms. Nelson, your husband is here." The front desk clerk walked in. I frowned my face just hearing that Melvin was out front.

"Baby, let me call you back. I have to get to work." I lied.

"Aight. I'll see you later right?"

"Of course." I smiled. The moment I heard silence, I quickly hung up the phone. I let out the deepest sigh then proceeded to the front of the office.

When I made it to the front, Melvin stood there in his dingy plaid shirt and his eyes were red from the liquor. I shook my head because this nigga didn't give a fuck how he came into my job.

"What Melvin?"

"Don't what me, hoe. I was just making sure yo ass was here. You been acting different." he slurred.

"You are drunk. Bye ,Melvin, and please don't come here like this again. You're embarrassing."

"Embarrassing? All of a sud...sudden." he slurred. "Bitch, I got yo embarrassing at home." he shot nearly stumbling over. He looked like a straight wino and that shit was humiliating. I was glad everyone minded their business and pretended he wasn't here.

"Bye." I told him then walked away. I didn't have shit else to say to this nigga. I had bigger shit to worry bout like is my partner okay and my plan going smoothly.

When I got back into my office, I didn't feel like sitting in this place another minute. Grabbing my purse and suitcase, I headed out the door to my man. I wasn't the pop-up type but since we were now official, I didn't see anything wrong with it. Sooner or later, we'd be together and living well off. I walked towards the door and went to turn off the lights. Before I could, a officer by the name of Lequan busted into my office.

"Ms. Nelson. Sarg is trying to reach you. He said you need to get down to Andrew's asap." I looked at Lequan and in an instant, my heart fell into the bottom of my Miu Miu pumps. I already knew what Sarg meant by *ASAP*.

21 / MERCEDES

I WALKED up to Brent's front door with my bat and mace ready to pop off. This nigga had me fucked up. It's been a couple months since I'd seen him and this nigga hasn't answered my calls. I already knew what this was about. More than likely he had him a new bitch because he always went MIA on me. Yes, I had shacked up with a new nigga but that nigga turned out to be a coke head and a fraud. When I met he he swore he had paper but come to find out he was a ordinary corner boy working for the next nigga. Y'all know me, I shook his ass and now here I was back to claim my nigga.

Bam! Bam! Bam! Bam! Bam!

I beat on his door and waited for him to answer. I knew his ass was here because his 64 Impala was out front and the top was down. After waiting for some time he never came to the door so I went around back. When I got to the back door, I heard a girl yelling and crying. I opened the door shaking my head because this nigga was slipping. When I walked into the home, I stopped in the kitchen so I could eavesdrop.

"But why did y'all have to kill him?!" the girl cried.

"Man, I told you I ain't do that shit!"

"This shit has BME written all over it!"

"But what that gotta do with me?"

"Nigga, them yo boys."

"Vee. Come on, ma; you know I don't fuck with them niggas like that." Brent said blowing me back. This nigga was a straight lie for whoever this bitch was. He was a part of BME. Hell, he wasn't a worker. Nigga was a partner.

"Well, he's dead now and he was innocent in all this." the chick began crying again.

"A nigga love you ma. I would have never did no shit like this."

"Love you." I mumbled to myself. Oh this nigga really had me twisted. I stepped from inside the kitchen and waltz over to where they stood. The chick's back was to me, but Brent stared dead into my eyes.

"So, this the bitch you been dissing me for?" I crossed my arms over the other.

"Man, what the fuck you....."

"Veronica?"

"Hello, Mercedes." She had the nerve to smirk.

"I know you ain't fucking this hoe."

"I see we have the same taste in men?"

"Bitch!" I rushed towards Veronica but I was unsuccessful. Brent grabbed me by my throat and slammed me into the ground.

"Forreal Brent?" I looked at him as he stood over me. "So you choosing this bitch over me?"

"Girl, you got a lot of nerves. Don't you got a baby by his homie?" Veronica added from the sideline.

"Didn't you fuck his homie?" I screamed trying to get out of Brent's hold. I swear if this nigga let me go, I was gonna beat this bitch ass again. I already beat her ass once over my baby daddy and I'm sure she remembered. Brent was her savior today but the moment I caught this hoe it was on.

Finally getting out of Brent's hold, I stood to my feet and fixed my clothing. I looked from Veronica to Brent then back to Brent. I ain't gonna lie, my little heart was crushed. Yes, I've done things I shouldn't have and yes I didn't take Brent seriously; well at first, but I was in love with him. The only reason I had distanced myself for a while was because of the heat BME had caught with that ship confiscating their drugs. I had enough heat on me so a bitch had to lay low and that's when I met the coke head bum.

"So this yo bitch now?" I asked him half choked up. I tried so hard not to let the tears fall. Fuck that; I wasn't crying in front of this bitch. Period.

"Yeah, this my girl." I looked at this nigga to see if he was serious and he was.

"Yeah, aight." I nodded my head. I walked away from Brent and let myself out. I wasn't about to make a fool of myself. I've done that enough with Major. *Fuck these niggas,* I thought to myself. However, I will tell y'all this, I was still gonna beat the shit out of Veronica. One way or another.

Candy

Sitting in this cell, I was about to lose my mind. The judge denied my bail so I had to just sit and wait. To be honest, I didn't give a fuck because that bitch Jas deserved everything I gave her. Not only did I hit a main artery in her arm but the bitch also lost her job due to injury. Yanese had come visited me a few times so she gave me the scoop on everything outside. She put money on my books and even had my baby. When I say I wasn't fucking with Trig, I was dead ass. That nigga was dead to me in my books. I hated I had to deal with him on business, because, had I not, I'd cut his ass off completely. Speaking of, I needed to call this nigga to check on my money.

I walked out my cell and headed to the phones. On the way, I bumped into this this Hispanic chick named Carmen that was my celly when I first arrived. Carmen had caught a case for having a burner so she was put in the shoe for a few months. She was cool as hell and I took a liking to her. We talked for a moment then I walked over to the available phone. I needed to holla at Trig asap.

"This is global tel link, you have a prepaid call from, Candice. To except charges press five. To deny charges press zero."

I waited for about two minutes then I heard Trig's voice.

"Hello?"

"Did you pick up from Brinks and Flocks?" I asked getting right to the point.

"Damn, hi to you, too."

"Just answer the question."

"Man, stop playing with me CeCee."

"Trig, just answer the fucking question so I can let you go."

"You ain't never letting me go. This shit to death Candy."

"Hump." I responded nonchalantly.

"Man, listen, this attitude shit is out the window. I was only there because I had to watch my daughter."

"Nigga, you was in yo fucking draws and the bitch was there!"

"She had just come back. That's why I believe what you saying about her doing that hit to the shop."

"So why you didn't let me kill the bitch?" I shot not giving a fuck if the call was recorded or not.

"I couldn't let you do that ma."

"Exactly my point. Nigga, you ran to the bitch aid! It really don't matter, Trayon. We had this conversation already. All I called about was my money."

"That's all you care about?" he asked trying to sound all sincere and shit.

"Yes, nigga! Just make sure my shit there when I get out. Anyway, what's up? You checked on my daughter?"

"Yes, I checked on *our* daughter. She good. And nothing is up. I'm getting dressed to head to the party." He said referring to the BME annual party. A part of me felt sad. Other than my child, this the one thing I didn't want to miss.

The annual BME parties were always lit. Every thot from 18-50 years old were there. Shit, I was sure with just enough sexy, girls under age got through security. Everybody in NY wanted to be in attendance. We popped bottles, had the baddest strippers, and we had all the money in the entire club. My boys were sexy. All of them in their own little way.

"Well, I'll let you go." I said in a jealous rage. I slammed the phone down and stormed off.

I walked to the tables and took a seat. I couldn't wait till time came for us to go to our cells. Since I'd been here I didn't fuck with nobody. Being a part of BME had me on my hi-horse. My books were fat, my case alone let bitches know I wasn't no joke and every woman in the whole facility wanted the inside scoop on my empire. These bitches were only digging for gold and looks though. So I wasn't worried by far.

When I first got here, one chick asked about Trig not knowing I was his wife. I brushed her off with a "Trig ain't shit." and kept it pushing. I wasn't bout to hate on bro; I was already into enough bull-shit over him.

"Dulce!!!" Carmen added emphasis calling my name in Spanish.

"Hey, Carmen." I smiled. I liked Carmen. She was always in a good mood despite her incarceration for killing her husband. This girl was looking at life but with the help of her attorney she was banking on *Alienation of Affection.*

"Girl, I just almost had to beat Big Kim ass."

"Y'all always beefing yo."

"Hell, yeah, she thinks because she's big she run shit."

"That's right ma. Don't let no hoe punk you or even attempt. But you know you can always come to me. I ain't scared of no extra case for you." I spoke on some real shit. These bitches thought Carmen was a pushover because of her niceness. A bitch couldn't even be nice without people thinking you were a punk."

"Fuck her. But what's up with you? Why the long face Mija?" I sighed.

"Same shit."

"Pinche Trig." She shook her head looking away. She was about tired of my Trig stories as I was, but she always listened.

I began telling her about our conversation and the party tonight. After we talked, we headed to our cells. I contemplated calling Yanese but I didn't want to bother anybody. I knew everyone was getting ready for the party so I simply picked up a book. I began reading A Hustlas Wife because it was my favorite book. I knew sooner or later I would be passing out with thoughts of Trig. As much as I hated that nigga, I couldn't front, I love him like Lil Wayne's daughter loved YFN Lucci. A real life love and lust. And even though I knew we might eventually find our way back, fuck that nigga right now. I was heartless.

Sigh.

"Hey, Marco, it's Peters."

"Nigga, I know who it is. Make it quick. I'm getting ready for the party." I said annoyed by this nigga's call. Peters was aight, I guess, however I just hated pigs period.

"Yes, I understand. Well, I'm calling you in regards to a Philip Mason."

"Who?" I asked puzzled.

"Philip Mason. A young kid that was murdered in Atlanta." The moment he mentioned the name, I looked up to make sure Morgan hadn't heard a word.

"What about it?"

"Well, the DA has you under investigation for the murder. I have to look further into it and because it's not my case or district it's hard. But, apparently, they have tied you to the girl and the evidence is a bracelet that was found with BME covered in diamonds." I looked down at my risk as if the bracelet would appear. I had lost it months ago but I never knew where. *Damn, that's where I lost it.* I thought.

"Good looking, P. But make sure you handle that shit my nigga." I said more of a threat than a demand. This nigga was making way too much fucking money to have even let shit get this far. Anything connected to BME was supposed to be taking care of.

"Baby, everything okay?" Morgan asked worried. I looked at her and contemplated actually telling her but quickly thought against it. Morgan couldn't handle no shit like that. This would break her for sure.

"Everything good baby. Go grab yo purse, let's roll." I kissed her forehead then patted her ass when she stood up. My baby was looking good as fuck in her all white Christian Carter dress I had copped her. A nigga spent three bands on that half-naked shit, but I couldn't front; she wore it well.

"Ding!"

My phone went off letting me know I had a text. Since my phone was already in my hand, I looked down to open the message.

Dizzy: *Since you stopped fucking with me for my friend make sure you tell her she's about to be a step mommy.*

Me: *bitch stop playing with me*

Dizzy: *oh you think it's a game? We'll see in 9 months. Congrats daddy!*

Me: *bitch I'mma kill you and that baby*

"I'm ready, baby," Morgan walked in damn near scaring me. I felt like I had been caught. This bitch Nana had a nigga fucked up. I swear if Morgan left me because of this hoe I was killing the bitch. And if Morgan thought she was just gonna leave me then her ass would be joining her friend. Straight up!

—

Pulling up to the party, I had so much on my mind I damn near wanted to stay home. Normally, I'd be pumped up over this event, but after the two bombshells I received, a nigga was sick. In two occasions, I had been caught slipping. I swear I had strapped up with

Nana so I was unsure of that situation. But, I still had that *what if* mind frame. That was only a part of my worries.

This shit Peters was talking had a nigga ready to skip town. All the shit I've ever did in my life, I was careless with knocking down Morgan square ass friend. On my granny, they was gonna have to kill me before I went to jail. I did four years in the pen and that shit was for the birds. I wasn't used to nobody telling me what the fuck to do, and I wasn't gonna ever get used to it.

"Baby, you sure you good? You seem kinda off." Morgan asked bringing me from my daze.

"You know I love you right?" I looked her in the eyes.

"Yes. Well, I think." she spoke unsure. I had never told Morgan I loved her but right now just seemed like the right time.

"Well, I'm telling you now, I LOVE YOU!"

"I love you, too, baby but you're scaring me." She looked worried. "Please, what's going on?" I swear I almost told her everything. I wanted her to be prepared when this shit hit the fan, but I still chose against it.

"Nothing, baby, damn. I just wanted to tell you I love you. Now, let's go party." I grabbed her hand and quickly pulled her out the limo.

Morgan and I wasn't in the party five minutes and already I almost had to slap two different bitches. Bitches didn't understand how to respect when I was in public with my shawty. I could understand that they were not used to me being in a relationship but damn I didn't belong to them either.

"Hey Marco." Tiana walked by flirting with a nigga.

"Bitch, keep walking." Morgan got buck.

"Chill, baby; fuck these bitches." I wrapped my arms around her. We walked upstairs to the VIP where our tables were. First niggas I spotted was Brent and Trig. I shook my head because this nigga Brent had about 48 hours to live. This nigga was acting weirder than before and it was about that time. It's been months since we put the nigga on this job and he was bullshitting. Had it been me, that bitch would have been dick downed then swimming with the fishes. But this tender dick ass nigga couldn't get the job done.

I walked over to Trig and took a seat by him. I needed to tell him about what Peters told me, although I knew he was gonna be upset. Now the bullshit with Nana, I was taking that shit to the grave. I just hope like hell she wouldn't spread the shit around the whole New York.

Morgan

I swear these disrespectful ass bitches was trying me tonight. No, I wasn't turnt up, but I wasn't no punk either. I had no problem with getting these hands dirty and especially over my nigga. I looked over at Marcell as he sat and talked with Trig. I could tell something was bothering him but for some reason he wouldn't open up to me. Ever since I'd gotten with Marcell, shit been crazy. Me and my best friend were distant, I lost my other best friend back home and not to mention, I've figured out I was in fact sleeping with the enemy.

For the past few weeks, I have been contemplating on telling him who I was because I had a feeling I'd regret it later. Everything began to fall in place the day of the BBQ. The moment I laid eyes on Yanese, it all registered. One day, I asked Cambree if I could borrow her phone because mines had died. When she handed it to me, the screen displayed a pic of Yanese. I asked her who it was and she told me to mind my business. Then, one day, I came to visit and I noticed the tattoo that read Boss on her hand, which told me that it was more than likely Camiya's father.

See, Cambree wasn't the sleep around type of chick so for her to have had the name tattooed, I knew he meant something to her. On several occasions, I heard the name BME but I never knew what it meant. Piecing everything together, I realized, Boss Major is Cambree's baby daddy and Yanese's husband. Boss Major is also the leader of BME, whom I investigated and found out that he was the cause of Camiere being behind bars.

Every night, I wanted to tell Marcell I was Camiere's little cousin, but I didn't know how he would take the news so I chose to tell him at a later date. For the first time, Marcell told me he loves me and that made me feel more entitled to tell him the truth, however I didn't know how.

I didn't know the full content of the whole BME thing with my cousin, but I was afraid he'd look at me as an enemy. I knew enough to know that, when certain territories had beef, anybody associated was an enemy. I just prayed he'd understand I didn't know who he was nor that my cousin hated BME.

Camiere was another thing. I knew when he found out I was with a BME member, he would lose it. But just like Cambree needed to mind her business, I wasn't gonna let Camiere stand in the way of my love life. Plus, he was in jail for probably the rest of his life so all he could do was scream down my throat over the phone. Which was fine with me because nothing would make me stop loving Marcell.

"You enjoying yourself?" I turned around to see who the hell was standing so close to me that their lips were touching my ear. I slightly jumped when I realized it was Brent. On several occasions, when I was out with Marcell and his crew, Brent would always give me these googly eyes in a very flirtatious manner. Scared that Marcell would flip out, I kept it to myself.

"Um, yea..yes," I replied nervously as I stepped out of his reach.

"What you running for? I ain't gone bite ma." he stepped closer to me again. "What, you scared of Marco? Man, he ain't worried 'bout you; he prolly somewhere with one his bitches." He said causing me to look around. Marcell had walked off to talk to someone and basically disappeared into the crowd.

"What up Morgan?" Trig asked walking over. He looked at Brent suspiciously then looked back at me.

"Umm, nothing. Where is Marcell?"

"He went to holla at our peoples." he responded eyeing me. Brent must have felt the tension because he walked off as if nothing ever happened.

"What's up with that nigga?" he nodded his head in the direction Brent walked off.

"He asked me where was Marco and I told him I didn't know." I lied.

"Yeah, aight, well stay away from that nigga, ma. He bad for business." I nodded my head then walked over to take a seat. I looked down at my phone and noticed I had a iMessage.

Nana: *hey Morg. you at the party?*
  Me: *yes are you coming?*
Nana: *yeah I'm on my way*
  Me: *okay.*

I slid my phone into my clutch and sat patiently to wait for Marcell. Looking around the club, I was jealous because of what Brent had said. I knew Marcell had plenty female friends and I also knew there were a few here tonight. *I swear if this nigga somewhere with a bitch I'm catching a case,* I thought taking a sip from my drink. Moments later, him and Trig walked back over to our table but he didn't say a word to me. Instead, he took a seat and pulled out his phone.

Since we left the house, his phone had been going off constantly; something that it always did. At times, I wondered if Marcell was cheating on me because he was always gone and leaving me in his home alone. If I did find out, I would feel like a complete fool. I basically disobeyed my parents and my cousin to be with him.

Since the day Marcell showed up to my school, I'd been with him ever since. My parents called my phone ninety going north and they even had Cambree blowing me up. I knew when they finally caught up to me all hell would break loose, but, I was willing to take that chance. I loved Marco with every ounce of me and every day, my love grew stronger. I had finally gotten him to open up to me and even stop being such an asshole.

Finally looking over at me, he smiled and that made me feel better. I sighed to myself because I now felt a sense of relief knowing he wasnt upset with me. Taking another sip of my drink, I began dancing in my seat. Because I hadn't been out in so long, I was gonna try to enjoy the night.

Feelings, so deep in my feelings
   No, this ain't really like me
   Can't control my anxiety
   Feeling, like I'm touching the ceiling

I was in my own little world singing Ella Mai Boo'd Up when Marcell came and sat next to me. He began kissing on my ear lobe. Like a school girl, I giggled shyly feeling like the luckiest chick in the room. Marcell was fine as hell and because of his status I was sure every girl in the room wanted his ass. Hell, every chick in the room wanted anybody from BME they could get their hands on. These chicks were so thirsty, they stood on the opposite side of the rope praying they would be noticed. Security had the VIP section secured and thank God because there were already enough women in the section. And not to mention the strippers that danced naked freely.

"Marco, I love you." I snuggled up under his arm.

"Marco?" he laughed. He wasnt used to me calling him that but

he let it slide. "Yeah, ma, you got a nigga Boo'd up." he laughed referring to the song.

"I'll Boo Up with you forever too."

"Yeah?" he questioned unsurely. "Shit, I hope so." he replied then
took a hit of his blunt. He then looked out into the crowd with a look I
couldn't read. Something was on his mind and sooner or later I would
get to the bottom of it. I just prayed like hell it wasn't about me.

"Babe!" I called out for Yanese for the tenth time.

I went into our bedroom then into the kids' room and still no sign of her. I headed into her office but she wasn't in there either. I could tell she had recently worked because she had pictures and papers scattered all over her desk. I walked over to the desk and something caught my attention. There were pictures of my ex Cambree. I picked up the pictures and they looked recent. I stared at Cambree's picture for quite some time. She was just as pretty as I remembered her.

"*Damn,*" escaped my lips just watching her in the yellow dress she wore with her hair now blonde. She had picked up a little weight and it looked damn good on her. I moved on to the next picture and I damn near choked. She was holding hands with a little girl that wore long pigtails. Just like I had done Cambree, I stared at the little girl long and hard. I knew my eyes weren't deceiving me but this little girl looked just like a nigga. Keeping it one hunnit, she looked like a split image of Blessin. Now the question was, how the fuck did Yanese get a hold of the photos? I began rummaging and bingo! It all made sense; her ass was following Cambree, which meant Cambree was here in town.

"What are you doing?" I turned around to the sound of Yanese's voice. She stood there with a scared look and we both were silent.

"Yanese, please explain to me why the fuck are you following this girl around? Every last picture is a different day and location." I shook the pictures in my hand to let her know she was caught. She tried to snatch them but I pushed her back.

"Why the fuck you snooping through my shit?"

"You gotta be fucking kidding me. You knew this whole time I had a fucking kid?" I yelled ignoring her question. She dropped her head. "That's not shit you just keep from a nigga."

"I didn't want you to know!" she screamed. I looked at her as the tears welled up in her eyes. Any other time, the shit would have made me submissive, but nah, not this time. This shit was foul as fuck. I understand the way she feel about telling me Cambree was back but me having a child and not telling me was foul as fuck yo.

"My nigga, this my fucking seed we talkin bout. You caught up in yo fucking feelings but remember you was fucking the next nigga. You almost had a baby by that nigga, too! Or did you forget?" I ran up in her face. I know I hurt her with that last statement but it was true.

"I don't want this fucking baby to be yours!" she matched my tone, however this shit was breaking her. Tears streamed down her face, but I couldn't let Yanese break me. This was an innocent child we were talking bout. I didn't need any of my kids thinking I was some MIA dead beat. I was gonna see Cambree one way or another whether Yanese liked it or not. If this really is my baby, then shit, a nigga got some making up to do.

"Well, that's not your call." I said to Yanese then stormed out the room. I headed into our bedroom and grabbed my car keys.

A nigga was looking fresh to death and was ready to party. It was the night of the BME function and Yanese wasn't about to fuck up my mood. I was gonna enjoy myself then worry bout this shit tomorrow. Well, at least I hoped so because this shit was heavy on my mind.

I sat in the back of my limo so caught up in a daze I didn't even pay attention that we had arrived. I stepped out the whip and stopped to take in the scenery. There were cars, people and cameras everywhere. Feeling like that nigga, I smirked then headed into the club I now owned called *Bosses*. Impressed with the entire set up, I had to admit my moms did her shit. She had decorated the club along with her team and it totaled out to nearly a quarter of a mill. Tonight was really important for BME so every year we went all out.

I walked through the crowd getting daps from everyone who I fucked with. Everyone else pretty much watched in awe as I moved through the crowd. I had two twin Berettas on each side of my Russian Sable fur coat. I was ready for some shit to pop; especially how I was feeling right now. This shit with Yanese and Cambree had a nigga on the edge. I didn't mean to hurt Yanese but shit now she see how it felt. She was about to marry a nigga and actually thought my baby was his. Every time she told me the baby was Cam's, a nigga heart broke more and more. A nigga don't really wanna relish on the past so y'all gotta read *A Thugs Worth*.

Yanese and I had been doing to good and living great. I knew this baby shit could put a dent in our marriage, I just prayed it didnt.

"Boss!!!!" Brent fake ass yelled out. I headed to our section and joined my team. Everyone was here but Candy and Yanese who was on her way. Candy was still locked up fighting an attempted murder with no bail. The minute they gave her a bond she was out that bitch no matter the cost.

You can't reach me (what?), space coupe like E.T
  It's the plug tryna call me (skrrt, skrrt)
  I was up trappin' early in the morning (plug)

We held our bottles in the air and turnt up to "Plug Walk". Everybody was on they boss shit with the furs and we had a VIP full of bad bitches. Since Yanese wasn't here yet I got a few lap dances from some strippers because I was feeling good off the XO Remy and Dom P that was flowing through my system. Everybody that was in the entire club wanted to be in our section. Hell, everybody in the club wished they were a part of BME. But that wasn't happening. We were like a secret society and it was hard to get in. We had the money, the power and the world was in our hands. We had all the guns and drugs that were being shipped straight from Columbia. Every small time and even big time niggas got they work from us. Even the people that didn't cop from us, they connect did.

Every piece of dope being sold in NY came through BME. It was crazy how our empire formed; all because my slick ass wife. I had to give it to Yanese, she did that *hands down.*

"I'm telling you this nigga right here on some weird shit." Marco learned in. I looked up to see who he was talking bout but I knew. Brent.

"Yeah, that nigga ain't to be trusted."

"I'ma kill that nigga and that's on my granny." Marco said with so much hatred.

"Yeah, that nigga have been moving funny lately."

"Man, I think he falling in love with that bitch." he said referring to Veronica. This nigga was sent to lure the bitch in but he still hasn't got the job done.

"That nigga in love with that bitch. I'm telling you, Boss, just let me pop that nigga."

"Handle that nigga Polo." We clinked our bottles together then took a swig. There was nothing else to be said.

Marco slid over to attend to his girl. I really liked her for my nigga. She was classy, quiet and minded her own business. I had only met her a couple times but my gut instinct told me she was the one. I had never seen my little nigga so open for a chick so I was hoping little mama didn't fuck over him.

"I hope y'all niggas plotting on what I'm plotting on." Trig walked up holding his bottle. Before I could respond, something piqued my interest.

"Morgan, have you lost your...." she paused and looked over at me. We locked eyes, and it was like the club stood still. Time fucking froze. It's been years since I saw her and here she was in the flesh. *How the fuck she know Morgan?* I thought to myself but that was a conversation that had to be saved for later. Right now, I needed to holla at baby girl and see what it was.

"Cambree, what are you doing here?" Morgan asked but Cambree was too focused on me. Moving her eyes from Morgan she focused in on me. I was burning a hole threw her which was what made her look over.

"Major." she silently whispered. I stood to my feet and walked over to her.

"Let me holla at you." I pulled her arm so I could take her into my office. I needed to know about this kid that was possibly mines. She looked back at Morgan but I pulled her ass forward.

30 Mins Before...

"What Nana?" I answered the phone annoyed. I knew she was calling to drop dirt on Morgan and that shit was starting to bother me. I mean they were friends so why did this bitch feel comfortable with telling on her friend.

"Cambree, I know where Morgan is at."

"Nana, I'm trying to figure out why the fuck do you make it your business to always tell me where my cousin is and what she's doing? I thought that was yo girl."

"She is my girl and that's why I'm telling you. Look, do you wanna know or not?"

"Bitch, don't get smart," I could hear her smack her lips. I was ready to go off on her little ass but what she was gonna say was important. My mother and aunt were worried sick about Morgan. Her mother had called and said she never came home from school one day.

"She's at the BME party." Nana spat stopping me in my tracks.

"BME?" I asked as if I didn't hear her.

"Yes, BME. she goes with the boy Marco from BME and their having their annual party tonight.

"Where's this party at?"

"It's at a club called Bosses." she responded and before she can finish I hung up. I jumped up to put on my shoes then grabbed my purse to head out. I prayed like hell I could get in and get out without running into Major.

━━

And now here I was standing frozen in Major's office not knowing what to say. We stared at each other for so long my stomach began to turn. I know I was wrong for this and my brother would kill me, but this man was still as sexy as the last time I'd seen him. It's like every feeling I ever had for him came rushing back. I still loved this nigga. Over and over I asked myself what would I do if I ever saw him again, and to be honest, I thought I'd just keep it moving along. However, that wasn't the case. The way he ordered me to his office told me something was up and the only thing it could have been was *Camiya.*

"You got something you want to tell me?" he asked finally breaking our stare down.

"I don't have nothing to say to you nore tell you. Now if you'll excuse me I have to take my little cousin home." I tried to walk away. He grabbed my arm for the second time tonight and spun me around to face him. We were so close, I could smell the liquor seeping from his breath mixed with spearmint gum.

"Cambree cut the shit ma." he screamed at me then turned around. He walked over to a winery in the corner, poured himself a drink then took a seat on his desk. "How old is she?" he asked.

"How old is who?"

"My fucking daughter!" he shouted causing me to jump.

"Major."

"Man, how fucking old is she?"

"She's 5."

"5." he repeated.

"What's her name?"

"Camiya Leigh."

"Damn, you couldn't even give her my last name? I mean, that's the least you could have did, since you kept my daughter out my fucking life for five years."

"What the fuck you expect? Nigga you tried to kill my fucking brother then set him up to go to jail."

"Man, I ain't set shit up. And your fucking brother was gunning for my crew. That nigga was about to kill two old innocent people!"

"You muthafuckas killed my little brother." I shouted getting upset.

"Your brother came for us. And correction, I didn't kill your brother Cambree. But all this is beside the point. At the end of the day, she's still my fucking daughter; you got a nigga out here looking like a fucking dead beat and shit."

"What the fuck was I supposed to do Major?" I burst out into tears. "You lead me to believe you loved me but the entire time you loved her." I was now sobbing.

"Man, I did love you." he spoke calmly in a low tone. He looked me in the eyes, and I swear he seemed so sincere. I shook my head in disbelief. "I gotta go." I tried to run out but once again this nigga grabbed me.

"Look, Cam, I apologize about everything. I didn't mean to hurt you nor bring harm to your family. I hate you had to be dragged in the middle of this shit but the fact still remains we have a child together." I didn't respond. I looked at him then slightly pulled my arm away. He finally released his grip and that was my chance to walk out. Turning to leave, the sound of his voice stopped me.

"Can I at least see her?" I turned around to face him.

"Crown Hotel." I mumbled then ran out. I cursed myself the entire way down the hall. I was so caught up in my feelings I forgot the initial reason for my coming. Now I felt like shit. Here I was about to scream down Morgan's throat for being in love with a thug and here I was, lusting over my ex.

Sigh.

Yanese

After the fight I had just had with Major I wasn't up for the annual party. The way he treated me tonight, it wasn't like he was gonna miss me anyway. Talk about feelings hurt; this nigga had me laying in bed crying my eyes out. I know I was wrong for holding this information from him but he had to understand my reasons. True, I didn't want him to have another child but that wasn't the case. No matter how much Major swore he didn't love that girl, he fell for her. The nigga even had her name tattooed. There was too much going on with our empire and King Cam for him to get caught up over a child with Cambree. I know that sounded selfish of me but it was true.

My phone began to vibrate alerting me I had a text. I quickly grabbed it praying it was Major telling me he's sorry. When I looked at the message, it was from and unknown number and it was a picture message. I opened the message and damn near fell out the bed. A fresh pair of tears began to fall from my eyes. It was a picture of Major and Cambree together. I could tell they were at the party because of all the people that surrounded the background.

Seconds later, another picture came through of him and Cambree. Only this time it was the back of them and Major was holding her hand as if he was pulling her away. I jumped to my feet and went into my drawer. I slid into a pair of sweats followed by a tank top. I located my Nike Huaraches and put them on just as quickly. I then walked over to my closet and grabbed my 40 Glock. Major had me fucked up as if he forgot who the fuck I was. I had something for the both of them. I grabbed my car keys and headed out the door.

Driving towards the club, I prayed like hell both of them were still there. I was doing nearly 100 MPH trying my best not to crash. I was so mad I couldn't even cry anymore man. The more I thought of the picture the faster I drove. And the more I thought about losing my husband, my heart broke. I came to a red light and as bad as I wanted to run it I stopped hard on my brakes making myself jerk in the process. The moment the light turned green a black SUV pulled in front of me and blocked my path.

"Fuck out my way!" I yelled out blowing my horn repeatedly. The car was moving so I tried to go around it. Before I knew it, another car quickly pulled on the side of the SUV blocking me in. Suddenly, four people in all black rushed my car with guns drawn. I wanted so bad to press on the accelerator but I was blocked in. I couldn't grab my gun because I knew for sure they would kill me. Panic took over me just as my door flung open and I was dragged out the car. I began screaming and kicking but it was pointless because I didn't stand a chance. The masked men threw me into the SUV and sped off.

"Take her to the bricks." One of the masked men spoke. For some reason, that voice sounded so familiar but I couldn't figure it out.

"Why are you doing this?" I asked hoping someone would say something and I would figure out who these men were.

"Shut up, bitch, and ride." the man in the passenger's seat shouted. I sat back quietly and prayed like hell I'd get a chance to grab my gun. The man on the side of me watched my every move so it was hard. I bit my tongue. I was seconds away from cursing this nigga out. I looked out the window and so many memories flashed through my mind.

A few days had gone by and I was still well and alive. Camiere had opened up more and was even being nicer to me. We talked about all kinds of things and I knew I broke the ice when I made him break out into laughter a few times. However, he still was wearing this damn ski mask and that shit was starting to creep me out. Camiere was cool as hell despite him having me here to kill me.

Damn, Camiere, I thought to myself. The thoughts were bitter sweet, however these niggas weren't Camiere. That man was in jail rotting. A part of me wished this was him kidnapping me for a second time because the last time I had survived. I knew deep down this had a lot to do with BME so I was a bit shaken. Thinking bout Major and the argument we had, I was sure he was at the party enjoying himself while I was here about to die. I couldn't front, despite the whole Camiere, Cambree and baby thing, Major and I lived a great life together. I was gonna miss him dearly if I didn't make it out alive.

Oh, my God, my kids? I thought on the verge of crying. I wasn't scared to die; I was scared to leave my kids behind. I knew Major would take great care of them, but that wasn't the case; they loved me unconditionally so me not being around would affect a major part of their lives.

"Come on, bitch." The door flung open and one guy snatched me out. I was so caught up in a daze, I never even heard the car stop.

Reluctantly, I walked into an old, worn down home that was on a quiet street. I wanted so bad to scream but I knew I'd die for sure.

Walking up the short stairs, we went into a bar door that was covered by a sheet. The house looked abandon on the inside and that shit made me really paranoid. Seconds later, I was escorted into a darkroom and slammed into a chair. One man began tying me to a chair while another stood by to keep watch.

"BME, fuck y'all!" I said my last words hoping I'd intimidate the men. One laughed but the other took it upon himself to let me know his true feelings.

"Bitch, BME gone be mines and my niggas pretty soon. We gone get rich off you, then kill yo whole crew. Dumbass." He said and began laughing. I laughed with his ass. Not because what he said was funny but because he was talking too much. Something else Black had taught me a while back. *"Gangstas move in silence Yanese."* and this nigga was a show off which told me he wasn't in charge.

"If you don't die first." I told him and laughed cockily. If these niggas didn't kill me soon, my crew would find me and murder every nigga involved. I had a strong team of niggas and despite the blow up between Major and I, I knew he was the one who was gonna come in guns blazing.

IT'S BEEN two days since the blow-up with Yanese and her ass was still acting stubborn like always. She hasn't been home or even bothered to call a nigga. I guess she needed her space so I was gonna give it to her. Right now, I needed to see what was up with my baby girl. I popped up on Cambree yesterday and she thought she was slick. She was at the hotel but my daughter wasn't. She had on some little ass shorts with her ass spilling out the bottom. I didn't pay her no mind because I was happily married. Despite the argument with Yanese, that shit didn't change my feelings for her.

I stayed around and talked to Cambree for a while and she filled me in on everything important about my daughter. I learned her name was Camiya and she was named after Cambree, which was Leigh. I asked her permission to change Camiya's last name and she was okay with it. I mean, at the end of the day, I wasn't to blame for not being in my child's life; Cambree was. Regardless of what happened with us in the past, that still didn't give her the right to withhold the information about me having a child. I wasn't one hundred percent cool with Cambree at the moment but for now I would let shit go so I could see my baby. Therefore, here I was again today pulling up to the hotel. Cambree wouldn't give me her number so I had to do a pop up. I just hoped I didn't pop up on some shit I didn't need to see.

When I got to the door, I knocked twice and waited for her to answer. Moments later, she came to the door wearing a robe and I could tell she was naked underneath. I'd be a damn lie if I said she wasn't looking sexy as hell. Her blonde hair fit her complexion perfectly and I could see her nipple rings through the robe.

"My baby here?" I asked trying not to look too hard. She didn't say a word; she just opened the door further inviting me in. I walked into the room and Camiya was in front of the TV watching My Little Pony. She spent around to look at me and her big pretty eyes looked shocked as hell.

"Daddy?" she said but more of a question. *Damn, she know a nigga,* I smiled.

"Sup, pretty girl." I scooped her up into my arms. I began tickling her and she burst out into laughter.

"Daddy stop." She was laughing so hard. I finally stopped and walked over to sit on the bed with her still in my arms. I noticed her clothing laying on the bed and Cambree's dress laid beside Camiya's.

"Where y'all going?" I asked looking over at Cambree.

"We was on our way to the mall."

"Well, you can go. I'mma stay here with her." I reached into my pocket and pulled out a knot of money.

"I don't need your money Major."

"Man, it ain't for you. It's for my baby." I shoved the money into her hand. "Take your time too because me and Miya bout to hit the pool and chill out."

"Look, you can't just come around and start demanding shit. We already had our day planned."

"Miya, baby, go finish watching TV and as soon as mommy done getting dressed we going to the pool. Okay?" I told Camiya ignoring Cambree.

"Yayyyy. I'mma find my bading toot." She ran off towards the closet.

"Look, Cambree, don't make this shit hard for me. I'm not trying to demand shit. I just wanna spend time with my baby. Is that a problem?" I looked at her to wait for an answer. She looked like she wanted to talk shit but to my surprise she shook her head no.

"Thank you."

"For what?"

"For making sure she know a nigga."

"What, you thought she didn't? No matter how much I hated you, I made sure to show her your pics every day." she said then brushed her hands through her hair nervously. I grabbed her hand and studied her tattoo. It said Boss with a crown. I looked up at her and it was like her eyes spoke volumes.

"You still love a nigga, huh?" I asked still holding her hand. I searched her eyes for the answer even though I already knew the truth.

"I'll always love you, Major Banks." She dropped her head. I stood from the bed right in front of her. I lifted her chin and made her look at me. Before I could express how I felt, Camiya barged back in.

"Daddy! Daddy! Daddy! I got my bading toot." She jumped into my arms. I looked at Cambree and she wore an embarrassed look. She quickly ran towards the restroom. I sat Camiya down on the bed then picked up her clothing. I walked to the restroom to hand Cambree her clothes because I knew she wouldn't feel comfortable getting dressed in front of me.

When I opened the door, she was naked in front the mirror. My eyes roamed her body and her shit was still sexy. She had light stretch marks on her hips which was weird because she didn't have any on her stomach. She quickly wrapped the robe around her body to cover up.

"My bad. I was bringing you your clothes." I handed her the dress. "And I don't know why you covering up; ain't like I never seen that shit before." I laughed then closed the door. Before I could make it to living area, she opened the door.

"You won't see it again!" she screamed out.

"Girl, you lucky my daughter right here." I shot laughing. I was just bullshitting with her though. I couldn't go there with Cambree. A nigga was faithful and real shit I didn't want to open those closed wombs. I know I hurt Cambree before so I didn't want to put her through that again. Me hurting her previously is the only reason I accepted this shit with Camiya. No, that wasn't a legit reason for her to do this so I used the shit with her brother as the main reason. Speaking of, that was something else I wanted to holla at her about. I knew Cam hated a nigga but how did he feel about me being Camiya's father? Shit, did he even know, is the question?

Cambree

I walked back into the hotel room and found Camiya and Major passed out on the sofa. I quietly picked Miya up and carried her into the room and laid her in the bed. I headed into the living area and began cleaning up the mess they had made. There was ice cream, Joe's Crab Shack trash and gummy worms everywhere. Once I was done, I walked over to Major to wake him up. It was nearly ten pm so I was more than sure he needed to get home. As much as I would have loved his company, I couldn't go back down that road. And not to mention he has someone at home waiting for him.

When I neared the sofa, I couldn't help but admire him. He was still so damn sexy. His shirt was off and he was only wearing his wet shorts and his socks. *This nigga done made himself comfortable,* I thought looking over at his shoes by the door. The sound of his phone ringing scared the shit out of me. Since I've been here, it rang multiple times. I wanted to wake him up but he looked so peaceful.

I walked over to where he was so I could at least put a pillow under his head.

"Ahhhh." I screamed out in laughter. "Let me goooo." I giggled.

"Nah, yo ass on some creep shit. You watching a nigga sleep and shit." He playfully bit my shoulder. I was laughing so hard I almost peed my panties. I fell back landing on his manhood and instantly it began to rise.

"Ummm." A moan escaped my lips that I didn't mean to let out. It's been so long since I felt the touch of a man my pussy got moist within seconds. Major thought he was slick. He kept me in the same spot and I could feel him slightly grinding. Next thing I know, his hand slid up my dress and he went straight to my pussy. Without warning, he slid my panties to the side and shoved his finger into my opening. I began rotating my hips matching the rhythm of his finger.

"Why this shit so tight ma. How long it's been?" he said into my ear. I could barely speak so it took me a minute.

"Since the last time. Ooooh."

"The last time me and you..."

"Yes, Major." he began to finger me harder. I laid my head back on his shoulder on a verge of cumming. I knew this shit was wrong but I wished he'd just fuck me right now.

He began kissing and sucking my neck to the point I could feel a hickey forming. Right when my nut was coming...

"Mommy, you okay?" I jumped up at the sound of Camiya's voice. Once again I was embarrassed so I ran off to the restroom. This time I locked the door.

Moments later, Major knocked on the door.

"Aye, ma, you good?"

"Yes, I'm fine!" I threw some water on my face then exited the restroom.

When I got to the front by Major, he was in the process of answering his phone.

"What?!" he jumped to his feet. "The fuck you mean?" he looked worried. "Man, I'm on my way." He hung up the phone shaking his head. I wanted so bad to ask was everything okay but that wasn't my place. He looked at me as if he didn't want to break the news that he was leaving but I was fine with it. I needed some time alone anyway. I needed to clear my mind because shit was moving too damn fast.

"I'mma see y'all tomorrow alright." He stepped up to me and kissed my forehead. He then used his hand to rub the side of my face. It was crazy because it seemed like he didn't want to go. I quickly broke the intense moment and he walked over to Camiya and kissed her as well. He promised her he'd be back and just like that he was gone.

I headed to the restroom to take a shower. I stripped out my clothes still on a high. When I climbed into the water, I let out a much needed sigh. Not being able to control myself, my tears began to pour down my face. I slid down into the tub and let the water wet me completely. Thinking bout Major, I cried hard. I cried, rocked my body back and forth; my heart was broken.

Again.

I PULLED up to Morgan's aunt's house because her ass wasn't answering her phone. She had been gone all day so a nigga was getting worried. I wasn't worried about her cheating on me; I was more worried she was back on a plane home. Ever since her big cousin showed up to the party she had been acting strange. I mean, I understand she felt like she was caught but fuck that, she was grown. Her parents had finally caught up with her so that was the reason she had left. She wanted to let her aunt know she was good. Whoever her snitching ass cousin was, Boss had baby girl sewed up. When I asked him who she was, he said it was a long story so I brushed her off as one of his old hoes. I knew my nigga too good; he never cheated on Montana and if he would have I would have been the first to know. No lie, though, she was bad as fuck. She looked like that *Love and Hip Hop Bitch* Alexis Sky with her sexy ass. Hell, yeah, I watched that shit. Every night I came home from hustling, Morgan had it on DVR recorded for a nigga.

Suddenly, the headlights to a car pulled up. I slightly ducked down so I wouldn't be seen. Hearing the car doors slam I lifted up to look across the street. Morgan had gotten out of a car and she wasn't alone. The driver jumped out and I focused in hard.

"*King Cam?*" I asked puzzled. Last I remembered he was locked up. I grabbed my strap ready to jump out. *The fuck she doing with this nigga?* I thought. *Damn, was she setting me up this whole time?* I questioned myself. This nigga was a fucking enemy.

I knew King Cam all too well. Shit, I was the one that murked his brother at the club. He hated BME, so, again what the fuck was she doing with him?

My phone rang knocking me from my thoughts. I looked at the caller ID reluctantly. Even though I had no plans on answering, I had to because it was Boss. The only time this nigga called me was when shit was serious or he was having problems at home. I didn't know why he confided in me because for so long I was single and a straight hoe. And if it was up to me, he would have been too. Nothing against Montana, I just didn't believe in love. Well then, because look at me now.

"Sup?" I answered.

"Nigga. Shit ain't right. I need you to meet me now at the spot."

"Everything good though?" I asked because I was in the middle of something. I was about to do us both a favor and body this nigga Cam.

"Is it about this nigga Cam?" I asked eagerly.

"Huh?" he answered with a question. That right there told me he didn't know this nigga was home. "Yanese, man. Somebody got her. They called demanding some bread.

"Whattt!" I screamed damn near shooting myself. "Say no more; I'm on my way." I hung up and headed to our meet-up spot. Just knowing something was up with Montana, had me on a real life high. I looked at her like a big sister, a mentor, a boss. True, Boss had taken over the empire, but Montana was the Captain. If it wasn't for her I wouldn't be where I am today. I was gonna go in gun blazing and even die for her if I had to.

Morgan gotta wait.

━━━

I pulled up to the spot but I had to take a detour. I don't know why but it was a weird ass car looking like they were trailing me. I knew it wasn't this nigga Cam because he hadn't seen me ducked off. When I pulled up on the side of the car, the man turned off into a subway parking lot so I kept it pushing.

I walked into the spot and Boss was at the head of the table which let me know shit was serious. This was my and Trig's *conference room* as we called it and Boss never interfered with how we ran shit.

I looked around and West was here along with a few other soldiers. *Where this nigga Brent?* I asked myself. But knowing him he was with a bitch. I couldn't wait to kill that nigga. He was dead weight in the squad. We didn't need that nigga and I was sure to handle him soon.

"What's up Boss?" I asked leaning against the wall. Fuck sitting down; I needed to be the first nigga to move.

"Shit crazy. Since I didn't answer my phone somebody called Trig talking bout they had Yanese. They asked for 3 mill and for me to bring it alone."

"Man that's a set up."

"Same thing Trig said. But I gotta go. I ain't gotta choice." He shook his head.

"The bread ain't shit but what if them niggas tryna kill you yo?"

"Shit, the nigga dies." Trig said like it wasn't nothing. I'm guessing because he had a bitch this was protocol.

Now that I was with Morgan I understood though. Right now I was ready to kill her and that nigga Cam so my frame of mind was *fuck a bitch.*

"Trig right. If I die, at least I protected my bitch. I can't leave her hanging. I'll never live with myself."

I looked at Boss. I wanted so bad to bring up this nigga Cam but that was more problems on top of the shit he was already dealing with. Just looking at my nigga, he looked stressed the fuck out and it was stressing me out to see him like this. *What if Cam kidnapped her again? I mean, he kidnapped her before. And how is it all of a sudden he's home, now she's missing.*

"So how we gonna do this?" Trig asked bringing me from my daze.

"Y'all just wait up the street in a unmarked car. But you two crazy niggas gotta be discreet. Once I get her to the whip safe we go back in that bitch blazing."

"I'm wit it." I said ready to make a move.

"We gotta wait until these muthafuckas call. They gone hit me with the location tomorrow. I got the bread with me in those bags." He nodded over to about ten duffle bags. *Damn 3 mill,* I thought shaking my head. Like I said, the money wasn't shit. I just hoped Montana was good and Boss made it out that bitch alive. "I'ma chill here so y'all niggas go get some rest. I'll hit y'all soon as it's time." he said kicking his feet up on the table.

"Shit, I'm staying here with you bro." Trig said then sparked a blunt.

"I'mma stay too, but I need to make a run real quick. Fuck it; we up all night." I gave Boss then Trig a pound.

I headed outside then pulled out my phone to call Morgan. Again she didn't answer and this shit was starting to frustrate a nigga. I jumped in my whip and drove straight to my crib to grab my chopper. This nigga Cam wasn't no threat but that nigga wasn't no bitch either so I knew I had to come correct. I rather been safe than sorry.

I quickly jumped out the car and ran into the house. I ran to the extra room where I had a hidden safe that held my straps. Before I could step foot through the door, I heard a loud thump that stopped me in my tracks. I ran to the hall to see if I seen anything unusual and a few red lasers caught my attention.

"Shit." I tried to run for the back door but by the time I made it, it was too late. They had my shit surrounded.

"Freeze!" about twenty officers shouted at the same time.

There was about sixty officers in total and they all had guns pointed at me. Looking amongst the crowd of crackers, I watched their body language and I could tell they wanted to shoot a nigga bad. They all wore ATF jackets and helmets with visors. At this point, I wished I had made it to my chopper because I would have went out with a bang. I knew I was gone for the rest of my life, and all because a backstabbing hoe.

Damn.

"So you have a baby by the nigga that put me in jail and expect me not to kill this nigga?!"

"Camiere, lower your tone please baby."

"Fuck that mama. You know this shit foul yo."

"But she didn't know. And she was already pregnant before you went." my mother tried to justify. I didn't care about shit they were talking about. That nigga Boss had violated. We could have settled our beef in the streets but this nigga wanted to play with the pigs.

"You fucking that nigga again?" I ran up on Cambree. She looked so scared like I was gonna hit her. "Huh? Answer the fucking question?" I shouted in her face.

"No I don't."

"You a muthafucking lie. Shit written all over your fucking face." I shook my head walking away from her. One thing I never did was put my hands on a woman, well except Yanese but she deserved it. I wanted so bad to slap fire from my little sister, but I couldn't bring myself to do it.

"Camiere, I didn't know I was pregnant though."

"You didn't even tell me when you found out. You had five fucking years to tell me this!"

"I didn't even tell him!" she shouted then burst out into a fresh set of tears. It hurt me to see my sister so hurt but the fact still remained this nigga had to go. For five fucking years, they hid that I had a niece running around. It didn't matter that she belonged to Boss; she was still my blood and I'mma gonna love her regardless.

Yesterday, I finally surprised my family with my being home. The only one who knew was my mom. The moment Camee saw me she instantly started crying. Other than Veronica and Kaliyah, Cambree was the one who held shit down while I was gone. She came to visit me and handled a lot of my business on the streets. Since I been home, I been laying low in the apartment Veronica had for me because I needed to get shit in order with that BME nigga Brent. Since Veronica's dumb ass decided to fall in love with the nigga I had to take matters into my own hands. After I killed Brent, I was gonna have to kill her because she knew too much and I couldn't trust her. Tonight was the night I was gonna kill him so I could move on to my next victim.

"Just please for me Camiere." Cambree cried as if she was reading my thoughts.

"Man, Camee. I can't promise you that."

"What about my baby?" We both looked towards the table where Camiya ate her pizza.

"She gone be straight," I told her because I had my niece no matter what.

"So she gotta grow up without a father like we had to?" She hit me with a gut punch. Instead of responding, I walked off towards my old room. I needed to get away from this girl before I became submissive. I understood how she felt, but she had to understand how I felt too. I spent years of my life behind bars over some shit I didn't do.

I sat in my old room at my moms' crib looking at the pic of Yanese and

I laying in the bed of our old home. I hated that my moms still kept shit like this around but it was her. She still had pics of my father and she couldn't stand him. I had a couple pics of Yanese that I had gotten from one of the guards. I don't know why, but I stared at the pictures on a daily. As much as I hated her, I still held onto the sweet memories. Yanese and I had some great times together and it was like she was meant for a nigga. She was sweet and innocent, just tainted by the streets. That girl didn't fit the lifestyle she portrayed; she was really forced into it. I couldn't put all the blame on Boss though, because her ex-husband played a big part. That nigga created something that would never be sane again. He turned a delicate flower into a delicate beast.

Now, I don't know if Yanese was in on Boss framing me but it really didnt matter. Real shit, something told me she had no clue but I couldn't spare her though. She had to go right along with that nigga Boss.

It was more to it than just her hurting me by sleeping with the nigga. It was about Lil Cam. she played a part in my his murder right along with her crew. It was impossible for her to have pulled the trigger because she was with me that night but her crew is the one who had killed him. She stood in my face and watched me cry but had never said a word. I understand she was forming her crew, but she was my bitch. I expected loyalty that I never got. The more I looked at her picture of her, the more frustrated I became. I hated the power she held over me and the shit was to obvious; Even Veronica could tell.

I dropped the picture of Yanese onto the bed then stood to my feet. I slid into my black hoodie and grabbed my two straps from the nightstand. I quickly made my way out the door hoping like hell I didn't bump into Cambree on my way out. Walking through the living room, everyone was gone but Morgan. She looked at me as if she wanted so bad to stop me from leaving but she knew not to get in my business.

Morgan was my favorite lil cousin and she knew it too. When she was younger, I pretty much treated her like my own child. Years down the line her mother and father sent her off to school and they even moved out there to be near her, so I didn't get a chance to see her often. I was glad though because she had a good head on her shoulders. She hated her parents had moved her away but what she didn't know, was, it was for her own good. Had she still been here, she would have been just like Cambree, in love with a street nigga.

"Be safe cousin." her big, pretty eyes pleaded. I nodded my head and walked out the door closing it behind me. Between her and Cambree a nigga was feeling soft. I had to get away from these girls. The way I was feeling right now, all I needed to do was run into Yanese and I'd prolly fold like a bitch. A nigga was too vulnerable right now. I couldn't wait to get to this nigga Brent and rock his top back so I can fall back into gangsta mode.

▭

I sat outside of Brent's crib for two hours before he finally came out. The way he was dressed made him look suspicious. I watched him get into a black old modern van and the driver pulled off slowly. I gave the van a few moments then I began to trail behind it. Because it was so late at night, there weren't many cars outside so I had to play it smart. I trailed the van onto the highway and we drove out about forty minutes away. When we finally pulled up, we were in Yonkers at a old abandoned house. *Fuck these niggas got going?* I thought watching them from the end of the block.

From where I sat, I had a plain view of them walking into the house. One man stood guard as they got out the van suspiciously. Moments later, the van pulled off and two men went inside including Brent. Because they were with Brent, I knew they had to be a part of BME which was fine with me because I'd kill three birds with one stone.

Once the coast was clear, I exited my whip and made my way towards the house. Because the house was old and worn down, it was most likely built with a underground attic. Quietly walking around the house, I found the tunnel to take me underneath. I pulled out my phone for light then brushed the few spider webs out my way. I then began to crawl using my elbows to guide me. The house was so old and the wood was so thin, I could hear a clear conversation coming from above. I could even hear footsteps throughout the house as people walked up and down what I assumed was the hallway.

"Shit!" I screamed out praying no one had heard me. There was a big ass rat just sitting in the corner as if he didn't have a worry in the world. Nigga had not ran off or nothing. Instead, he watched me just as I watched him. *I'mma shoot yo ass you come near me,* I thought crawling far the fuck away from him. I hated rats.

"Call that bitch ass nigga. When he get here we make him come to the door and we kill him."

"What if it don't work?"

"Nigga, it's gonna work. Trust me, he want his bitch so he's gonna bring the money."

"Well, call him, let's get this shit over with."

Just listening to these niggas had my antennas up. Now I was confused as to what they were gonna do. A part of me felt like maybe they were talking about me. Veronica had fell in love with Brent but it was possible he played her stupid ass. I could tell you this though, these niggas were dumb if for one second they thought I would pay to get the bitch back. Hell they were doing me a favor.

"Big J, go get the rental just in case we gotta hurry and get out of here."

"Nah ,I'm not leaving you my nigga."

"I'm good. I got Slim right here." Brent said referring to another BME member. *These niggas just made my job easier,* I thought laughing to myself. It was only two niggas in the house which was better than three.

I crawled towards the back but making sure to keep looking back for that damn rat. When I got to the end of the home, just like I thought there was a door that led upstairs. Because I was too tall to stand up, I crawled into the door then headed up the four steps that led to another door. Quietly opening the door, I peeked my head in to make sure the coast was clear. I then tiptoed down the hall praying I didn't fall through the ground. The house was raggedy as fuck. I entered the kitchen and I could see a flicker from a candle down the hall. I pulled out a penny from my pocket and threw it across the wall. One man ran towards the kitchen and when he entered.

"Thuuu!"

I rocked his ass to sleep with my silencer.

Holding the gun down to my side, I made my way down the hall and into the room. Brent had his back to me so he never saw me coming. There was a woman tied up to a chair but her head was down and her hair was flung in the front of her. Brent stood over her and slapped her so hard blood flew from her mouth. Because the light was so dimmed, I couldn't tell if it was Veronica or not. I stepped in further and Just my luck, the ground creaked causing him to turn around.

"Pop!"

He let off a shot hitting me in the arm.

"Thuuu! Thuuu! Thuuu!"

I let off two shots into his chest then one to the head dropping him instantly. Holding my arm, I walked over to Veronica and used my gun to lift her head. Her hair flew back exposing her bloody face. But it wasnt Veronica. I knew this face from anywhere. My eyes had to be deceiving me so I blinked a few times.

"Camiere?" she asked with tears pouring down her face.

"Yanese?" I asked puzzled. We stared at each other without saying a word. Her eyes pleaded for me and I'm sure mines did too. Just looking at her bruised face made my jaw clench. I rubbed my hand down my face and shook my head repeatedly.

Ain't this about a bitch!

To Be Continued!

SUBSCRIBE

Text Shan to 22828 to stay up to date with new releases, sneak peeks, contest, and more...

WANT TO BE A PART OF SHAN PRESENTS?

To submit your manuscript to Shan Presents, please send the first three chapters and synopsis to submissions@shanpresents.com

CPSIA information can be obtained
at www.ICGtesting.com
Printed in the USA
LVHW01s2042110718
583386LV00015B/1044/P